Mazaltob

Mazaltob
A Novel

BLANCHE BENDAHAN

Translated and Edited by
YAËLLE AZAGURY & FRANCES MALINO

Brandeis University Press
WALTHAM · MASSACHUSETTS

Brandeis University Press
© 2024 Brandeis University Press
All rights reserved
Manufactured in the United States of America
Typeset in PS Fournier by Stéphane Elbaz

For permission to reproduce any of the material in this book, contact
Brandeis University Press, 415 South Street, Waltham MA 02453,
or visit brandeisuniversitypress.com

LIBRARY OF CONGRESS CATALOGING-IN-PUBLISHING DATA
Names: Bendahan, Blanche, 1903–1975, author. |
Azagury, Yaëlle, 1970– translator. | Malino, Frances, translator.
Title: Mazaltob : a novel / Blanche Bendahan ; translated and edited
by Yaëlle Azagury & Frances Malino.
Other titles: Mazaltob. English
Description: Waltham, Massachusetts : Brandeis University Press, 2024. |
Series: The Tauber Institute series for the study of European Jewry |
Includes bibliographical references. |
Summary: "The novel Mazaltob (1930) by Blanche Bendahan
is the forerunner of a modern Sephardi feminist literature in French,
which in recent decades has earned growing recognition.
Yet this model for a vital current of post-colonial literature
has disappeared from our cultural memory.
Rendering the novel Mazaltob into English
aims to repair that loss"
— Provided by publisher.

Identifiers: LCCN 2023048011 (print) | LCCN 2023048012 (ebook) |
ISBN 9781684582068 (cloth) | ISBN 9781684582051 (paperback) |
ISBN 9781684582044 (ebook)
Subjects: LCSH: Jewish women— Fiction. | Sephardim— Fiction. |
Tétouan (Morocco) — Fiction. | BISAC: LITERARY CRITICISM /
Comparative Literature | FICTION / Jewish | LCGFT: Novels.
Classification: LCC PQ2603.E533 M3913 2024 (print) |
LCC PQ2603.E533 (ebook) | DDC 843/.912— dc23/eng/20231024
LC record available at https://lccn.loc.gov/2023048011
LC ebook record available at https://lccn.loc.gov/2023048012

5 4 3 2 1

To all young women whose freedom is elusive.

Contents

Preface

YAËLLE AZAGURY and

FRANCES MALINO

The novel *Mazaltob* (1930) by Blanche Bendahan is the forerunner of a modern Sephardi feminist literature in French, one which in recent decades has earned growing recognition. Yet this model for a vital current of post-colonial literature has all but disappeared from our cultural memory. Rendering the novel *Mazaltob* into English aims to repair that loss.

While Francophone literature in general has drawn attention following the publication of Edward Said's *Orientalism* forty years ago, Judeo-Maghrebi and Sephardi literature, in particular, retain only a discreet presence. With the notable exception of works by Albert Memmi and Edmond Amran El Maleh, this richly textured literature—which flowered in Morocco, Algeria, and Tunisia in the first half of the twentieth century—has remained largely unknown to contemporary readers, finding a home neither in Orientalist studies nor in Jewish studies. It has received only meager attention even in France. Nevertheless, its core themes—multi-layered identities, gender differences, feminism, the confrontation of tradition with modernity, and the place of Jews in colonial societies of the Arab world—continue to resonate with contemporary debates.

Why such neglect? The first obstacle has been methodological and epistemological. Despite common unifying features, both Judeo-Maghrebi and Sephardi literature do not fit the conventional boundaries of a national literature. Written in French, their stories often exploring complex and uneasy identities, these works struggled to find a suitable framework of reference, especially in Tunisia and in Morocco where profound changes in the culture arising from decolonization could not easily accommodate works that spoke of cultural alienation within their

Muslim settings. Those that built upon a national affiliation, as in the work of writers in Algeria—where most Jews had become French citizens since the Crémieux decree of 1870—were often put aside for ideological reasons, viewed as a "minor" production, and regarded with disdain by the "Métropole." To this day, they are generally considered inferior to canonical French literature.

In another dimension—the Jewish one—a different set of issues arises, as the stories recounted in these works often do not neatly fit the narrative of Jewish history produced by the dominant Jewish historiography. Though challenged in the last two decades, the vast scholarly field of modern Jewish intellectual history has been shaped almost exclusively by a European Jewish experience. It was informed by a teleological arc which begins in the late medieval ghetto, is then followed by emancipation and assimilation, the calamity of the Holocaust, and culminates with Zionism and the creation of the State of Israel. North African Jewish history markedly differs from that chronology. Countless works have thus remained underexplored or ignored at best. Few translations are available.

Ezra Pound's 1935 injunction, "make it new," put a name on a cultural and literary movement (modernism) that swept across North America and Europe subsequent to the horrors and absurdities of the First World War. While modernism has been abundantly documented in the West, little is known of its impact and ramifications in other parts of the world. The place of the avant-garde in the Maghreb, for example, in the early decades of the past century is largely uncharted territory. As for Sephardi modernist literature, to which we believe *Mazaltob* belongs, it remains for the most part undetected, or at best misunderstood.

Our translation (from the Latin *translatio*, which means "transfer"), however, is not merely a calque, a mechanical operation. Its etymology points to a "carrying over," whether in space or in time. Rendering a text in a different language is a balancing between the quaint, the alien on the one hand, and the familiar on the other. It is a delicate elucidation of words, a probing of the context, a delving into the historical moment and into the stances of the actors portrayed. In that endeavor, some aspects might seem troublesome, even vexing—in sum, unsettling to the contemporary reader. Ignoring Bendahan's changes in narrative voice, or her disconcerting play with different registers, or the surprising interlacing of different languages, might have resulted in a flattening of her universe. Translation must hold onto that residual foreignness. Yet, despite this, exposing the familiarities in *Mazaltob* also came easily. Transposed into current debates, Mazaltob's dilemmas still provoke ripples in our contemporary dialogues.

Our goal in collaborating as historian and literary scholar has been to retrieve fragments of a rich culture the written traces of which, swept aside by the turbulent tides of history, have been largely erased. Among them, *Mazaltob* is prized for its elusive narrative voice, its avant-garde blending of genres, and its nuanced rendering of the tensions between "tradition" and "modernity," all of which make it one of the more engrossing examples of both Judeo-Maghrebi and Sephardi modernist literature.

The introduction by Frances Malino provides both biographical context and a window into Bendahan's world.

The analysis of the novel by Yaëlle Azagury in the concluding essay ("*Mazaltob* and the Rise of the Modern Sephardi Novel") lays the foundation for and heightens the importance of a new field of Sephardi literary studies for works written in French and located in the Maghreb.

Tetouan. Photo courtesy of Ben Ragsdale/Diarna Geo Museum of
North Africa and Jewish Life, 2011

Introduction

FRANCES MALINO

Tetouan has lost its "uniqueness."[1] So bemoaned acclaimed poet, journalist, and novelist Blanche Bendahan. Bendahan was neither born in Tetouan, nor did she ever reside there for any significant period. Yet her intimate familiarity with the city's inhabitants and her vivid descriptions of its rich Sephardi culture—rooted in a place of deep affection—suggest that she claimed this luminously white city nestled against the Rif Mountains of Northern Morocco as her own.

Bendahan's award-winning *Mazaltob*, set in Tetouan at the turn of the twentieth century and first published in 1930, is a novel about the perils of boundary-crossing: those of gender, as a beautiful Jewish girl seeks to break the molds of a patriarchal society, and those of religion when she dares to love outside her religious community. It is about the uneasy transition to a new world and the changes, at times life threatening, wrought when the rigors (and comforts) of duty are challenged. It toys with new forms of writing, yet revels in the old. And it provocatively suggests replacing the idea of a single home and country—to which one can never fully return—with multiple homelands, spiritual as well as physical.[2]

Blanche Bendahan was well known in her lifetime; indeed she was featured on numerous radio broadcasts—"Judeo-Spanish ballads of the Sephardim," for example, on Radio-Alger—as well as in interviews and at conferences throughout Europe and the Middle East.[3] Yet she has remained an elusive figure. Even the date of her birth and her parentage are shrouded in mystery.[4] Archival investigation and recent scholarship have helped to solve some of these mysteries. A few, however, persist, tantalizing in their implications.

Blanche Jeanne Benoliel was born on November 26, 1893 in Oran, a port city in northwest Algeria just 266 miles east of Tetouan. She was a citizen of France, which had annexed Algeria in 1848 and in 1870, under the Crémieux decree, granted the majority of its Jews French citizenship. A "colorful and religiously diverse city," Oran was home not only to its minority Muslim population, but also to Europeans from Spain, France, and Italy, as well as Moroccan Jews, Judeo-Arabic-speaking local Jews, and Jews from Livorno. (In 1830, at the time of the French conquest, there were approximately 3,700 Jews in a population of 17,000.)[5] Once Jews from Tetouan arrived en masse during the Hispano-Moroccan war (1859–60) and Spanish occupation (1860–62), their influence on the language, cuisine, music, and literature of Oran's Jews stood unchallenged. As did the intimate ties they retained with their coreligionists in Northern Morocco.[6]

Blanche never knew her Catholic mother. Born in Malaga, Spain, Maria Fernandez died in childbirth in Oran at the age of nineteen.

Oran Synagogue.
Photo courtesy of
William Gross,
circa 1928

Introduction

Months later, her infant daughter was officially adopted by Hayo Alfred Benoliel (1872–ca. 1924), a Tetouani Jew born in Oran and no doubt Blanche's biological father. We know little of the relationship between Hayo and his daughter except that his appearance in *Mazaltob* suggests both warmth and appreciation.

On November 26, 1896, when Blanche was three years old, Hayo married Marie Hortense Ginoux in Marseille, France. It was to this Catholic stepmother, who "guided [her] childhood so tenderly," that Blanche chose to dedicate her "Jewish novel."[7] A dedication that nevertheless leaves unresolved if Blanche herself was legally Jewish, having been converted by a Jewish court of law.

Blanche spent her early years in France—Nice, Marseille, Paris, and Grenoble (a city "dear to [her] heart")—attending French schools and only returning to Algeria with her father at the age of fourteen. By then Hayo and Marie Ginoux had divorced.[8] At twenty-six, already renowned for articles and essays in Oran's journals and a prize-winning collection of poems (*La voile sur l'eau*), Blanche married Yahia (Gaston) Bendahan, a colonial goods merchant. Like her father, Bendahan was a Tetouani Jew and perhaps even a cousin on his mother's side. Little is known of their marriage (he was fifteen years older than she was and had been married once before) other than her attentiveness when he took ill. There appear to have been no children.

Blanche and her husband made their home in Oran, where she blossomed as poet and novelist, journalist, and political activist. In 1949 her *Poèmes en short* was unanimously awarded the Academic Prize of French Humor by France's prestigious Académie de l'Humour—only the second time since its establishment in 1923 that this prize was given to a woman. "Please read these poems," the noted French critic Paul Reboux advised, "you will understand why I enjoyed them so much. They are noble and classic, yet bursting with life. They are whimsical yet realistic, delicate yet ferocious, filled with irony yet also faith." No less enthusiastic was the president of the Algerian Literary Society, for whom the book was "light as a feather, but with the weight of a lively thought, sometimes womanly and sometimes manly, a combination of wisdom and talent." Both critics lauded the delicate and petite Blanche Bendahan—whom Reboux had first presumed was a man, the poems having arrived at his residence with only a contact address—for giving voice to the full human experience.[9]

Blanche's journal articles ranged over multiple subjects, including factories in Algeria, advances in modern medicine, and the beautiful vistas of Oran. She lectured on Islam, North Africa, and humor at the Sorbonne and the Emagine Theatre, was a member of the Union of Monotheistic Believers established in 1932 to bring Muslims, Christians, and Jews together, and established the French Culture Club as well as the Blanche Bendahan Award to encourage literary works whose settings were in Algeria. She herself was also the recipient of numerous awards, including *Officier de l'Instruction Publique*, *Commandeur du Mérite et Dévouement Français*, and *Commandeur des Arts, Sciences et Lettres*.

In 1933 Blanche became a founder and member of the executive committee of Oran's chapter of the *Ligue française pour le droit des femmes* (LFDF), a progressive suffragist movement committed to social reform.[10] It has been decided, the chapter announced in 1934, "to organize literary conferences with the aim of advancing women's rights." As "a woman of letters," Blanche was the first to be invited to speak. She chose as her subject the noted Romanian French feminist and novelist Anna De Noailles, who had died the year before.[11] Blanche presented again two years later, this time reading a selection of her own poems.[12] "In a largely male-dominated and anti-Semitic colonial society," the Algerian historian Saddek Benkada writes, "Blanche Bendahan emerged as a pioneering figure in the literary world, at the vanguard of both Jewish and feminist modernity."[13]

When Algeria gained its independence in 1962, Blanche left for France, as did most of Algeria's Jews. She published her final work, *Sous les soleils qui ne brilleront plus* (*Under the Suns That No Longer Shine*), in 1970, yet again garnering a prize, this time from the city of Nice.[14] A collection of essays (some having been previously published), *Sous les soleils* also includes a diary Blanche kept between November 8–12, 1942, when the Allies successfully attacked Casablanca, Oran, and Algiers. "That it was the Americans," she writes, "was the only hypothesis we had not imagined. It was the most unlikely. A miracle. Too beautiful to believe."[15]

Nostalgia and a deep sense of loss permeate many of the essays in *Sous les Soleils*, especially in Blanche's homage to the city of her birth—wistfully imagined as an Algerian Marseille "with its cosmopolitan allure"—and in the concluding poem tellingly titled *Retour au Sahara*.

> Other perfumes, softer perfumes, sometimes embrace us,
> But will they be infused with space,
> With that blessed purity?
> Scent of the South, unforgettable,
> White like death, red like life
> Without stain, without end![16]

Tetouan's Jewish cemetery looms large in Blanche's articles. Located on the hillside of Mount Dersa overlooking the old city, it is surrounded by hauntingly beautiful tombstones etched with delicate carvings. Here, she writes, rest the bones of ancestors from Castille, "a country never forgotten, mournfully loved, always loved, loved notwithstanding."[17] Unlike her protagonist whose name Mazaltob means good fortune in Hebrew, Blanche was buried in Nice on July 23, 1975, two days after her death.

Cemetery at Tetouan.
Photo courtesy of
David Cowles, 1993

xvii

Blanche Bendahan was thirty-seven years old when she completed *Mazaltob*. Published in Paris on the centenary of France's invasion of Algeria and republished in 1958 in Oran (there would also be two Spanish editions in 1997 and 2012), it was among the only novels written in French, declared the Jerusalem-born journalist and ethnographer Abraham Elmaleh, to describe the life of Maghrebi Sephardi Jews.[18] Journals and newspapers from both the right and the left, Algeria and the métropole, lauded *Mazaltob*'s realism, picturesque descriptions, and refutation of "false" observations. Bendahan's descriptions, the review in *La Renaissance Politique, Littéraire et Artistique* read, are a "far cry from the usual clichés on Morocco and the unbearably conventional chromolithographs that we have been fed."[19] In 1931 France's prestigious *Académie française* awarded *Mazaltob* one of its annual prizes. The only Jewish laureate among fifty-three (eight were women), Blanche Bendahan stood alone as well in having written on a Jewish theme.

Indeed, multiple themes—romanticism, antisemitism, colonialism, and the *Haskalah* (Jewish Enlightenment)—abound in this poetic tale of a beautiful and gifted Tetouani girl for whom liberation from a cherished yet suffocating world becomes a question of life or death.[20] A plea for religious pluralism, a feminist commentary, and the beauty of time-honored traditions inform the tale as well.[21] So, too, does an erotically charged atmosphere. It is a jewel of a novel, beckoning the reader to savor its richness.

Yet *Mazaltob* can also be read as an autobiographical journey, one in which Blanche Bendahan, much like the noted Tunisian-born Albert Memmi in *Pillar of Salt* (1955), navigates the continuities and ruptures of her own multifaceted and intricately textured life. Familial attachments as well as its unique history as a center of "*Séphardisme*" made Tetouan the perfect city for Blanche to situate this journey.[22]

Jews and Muslims alike had settled in Tetouan at the end of the fifteenth century, both having been expelled from Spain. They brought with them a pride in Iberian Renaissance culture, a fierce independence, and a determination—their keys kept close by—to return to their abandoned homes. Before long they transformed Tetouan into a thriving Mediterranean port city, designated by the Sultans as the place where foreign diplomats could establish consulates.

Introduction

Tetouan Synagogue. Photo courtesy of Ben Ragsdale/Diarna Geo Museum of
North African and Jewish life, 2011

Tetouan's Jews actively engaged in the rich commercial life of the city,
establishing trading networks with Sephardi communities in Leghorn
(Livorno) and Amsterdam, and with fellow Jews across Algeria, Tunisia,
and the Middle East. Under the guidance of Rabbi Hayyim ben Abraham
Bibas from Fez, Tetouan also became a major center of Jewish intellectual
and spiritual life.

As in most of Morocco, Tetouan's Jews lived apart in a separate maze of
narrow interconnected streets referred to in Tetouan by its Spanish name,
the Judería.[23] The language they spoke (*Haketía*), a fusion of fifteenth-
century Spanish, modern Spanish, Hebrew, and the Moroccan dialect of
Arabic, set them apart as well. Yet Tetouan's Jews and Muslims proudly
shared an Andalusian culture that permeated their music, cuisine, and
clothing, just as it choreographed their wedding customs and influenced
the architecture of their homes.

By the late eighteenth century, Tetouan's once thriving port was no
more, the Sultan having expelled all Europeans from the city. When
Sidi Muhammad b. Abd Allah subsequently welcomed the consuls and
businessmen back to Northern Morocco, it was to Tangier, the newly

designated diplomatic capital twenty-eight miles to the West. Wealthy Tetouani Jews, like the Benchimol family featured in Delacroix's portraits, soon left for Tangier. Blanche Bendahan's ancestors, however, remained in the city of their birth.

By the middle of the nineteenth century Tetouan's Jewish community numbered 5,340 in a city of about 35,000. The Judería boasted sixteen synagogues open to the public and more than ten rabbinical seminaries. The area of the Judería, however, first delineated in 1790, remained unchanged, despite petitions to enlarge it. Unchanged as well was the prohibition for Jews to build or live beyond its gates. Accorded protective status as *dhimmis*, as were all Jews and Christians living in the lands of Islam, they nevertheless remained subject to humiliating restrictions.

The Hispano-Moroccan war (1859–60) and the Spanish occupation of Tetouan (1860–62) permanently altered the city's fragile status quo, creating breaches between tribesmen and townsmen, Jews and Muslims, wealthy and poor. With Moroccan suzerainty restored in 1862, an increasingly more vulnerable Jewish population, having publicly identified its interests with those of the Spanish occupier, turned to Europe's Jews for protection.

On December 23, 1862, the Paris-based Alliance Israélite Universelle, established in 1860 by six young acculturated French Jews heeding the rabbinic saying *"kol yisrael arevim zeh bazeh"* (all Jews are responsible to

Tetouan's Judería. Photo courtesy of Frances Malino, circa 1910

one another), opened the first of its primary schools in Tetouan. Although records refer only to the male members of Tetouan's local Alliance committee, it enjoyed the active support as well of at least one woman: Blanche Bendahan's ancestor, Messody Coriat Benchimol.[24]

By the eve of World War I, 183 Alliance schools stretched from Tetouan in Morocco to Teheran in Iran. All shared a French curriculum modeled after that of the *écoles primaires* recently established in France, and all embraced the mandate of "vocational, spiritual and moral regeneration." By collectively labeling their students as "Orientals," all also incorporated the métropole's pejorative inferences of primitiveness and exoticism— attitudes Bendahan would both challenge and internalize.

Tetouan's Alliance school for girls (it opened in 1868, closed shortly thereafter, and reopened once again in 1882) plays a central role in Mazaltob's life. It is here she learns to read and write as well as to imagine, much to the annoyance of her fiancé José, that France's culture, history, and language might someday belong to her as well.

With the eye of an ethnographer, yet never succumbing to facile binaries, Blanche Bendahan captures in *Mazaltob*, as Shalom Aleichem did in his Tevye stories, a moment of upheaval and uncertainty, of traditions challenged and vistas enlarged. Yet in contrast to Shalom Aleichem, the issues Bendahan raises and the incidents recounted, seen through the lens of an avowedly feminist poet—humorous, satirical, dark, and always tender—find their historical resonance not in Eastern Europe, but rather in turn-of-the-century North Africa. As do, not surprisingly, the novel's central characters.

Early on, for example, we are introduced to Doctor Bralakoff, an Ashkenazi Jew loved by all "even if he was a *forastero* (foreigner)." Raising his nephew Jean as his son, the revered doctor plays a central role in Mazaltob's life, as well as that of her family. No doubt Blanche's model for this Western-educated, "modern" Jew was Doctor Jacques Berliawsky, an Eastern European Jew who arrived in Tetouan in 1891. A fervent Zionist, he intended to accept a position in Palestine. The Jews of Tetouan, however, "won" him over. "Everyone," he wrote to the Alliance in Paris during the summer of 1894, "is joyous that I am remaining."[25] Berliawsky kept abreast of the latest medical research (he spent time at the Pasteur Institute in Paris), understood the most radical techniques for treating croup and diphtheria, and corresponded with those advancing them. Amidst a raging cholera epidemic in 1894, Berliawsky, the sole doctor in Tetouan, extended his expertise to both Muslims and Jews.

Central to the novel are two interconnected themes that also have historical resonance in turn-of-the-century Tetouan: emigration in the odyssey of José, and early marriage in the betrothal of Mazaltob. Neither escapes Blanche Bendahan's critical eye. The lure of emigration had begun early in the nineteenth century, when a few hardy souls departed for Gibraltar and Oran.[26] Soon Tetouanis ventured farther, to Rio de Janeiro and Para (northern Brazil). Increasing misery and lack of opportunity in Tetouan led other young men to sever more fully the ties that attached them to their birthplace. In Caracas and Buenos Aires, they became haberdashers and traded in luxury items, directed large commercial houses, and established subsidiaries in the surrounding countryside. Their success, along with improvements in steam navigation, further fed the "fever of emigration." By the end of the century, more than one hundred Jews left Tetouan each year, a considerable number for a community of only six thousand.[27]

In all this, of course, Tetouan differed little from other cities and towns at the end of the nineteenth century where economic opportunity and desperation irrevocably transformed Jewish life. But in contrast to those leaving Eastern Europe, Tetouan's emigrants often returned, bringing with them the tastes and expectations of a more opulent life, along with a thoughtless dismissal of Tetouan's cultural and religious traditions. "The modern world will have to penetrate here even more," a young Tetouani woman complained, "for men to understand that disdaining religion does not demonstrate their superiority to others."[28]

Some emigrants also returned in search of a suitable young bride. Such is the quest of the novel's José Jalfon, a wealthy, middle-aged Tetouani Jew who enjoyed a hedonistic lifestyle in Buenos Aires.[29] To José, the beautiful sixteen-year-old Mazaltob is both elusive and to his liking. That her family has fallen on hard economic times only works to his advantage. As for Mazaltob, no one feels the need to consult her. "Civilization alone will make child marriage disappear," an Alliance teacher sadly mused when yet another of her students bid a sad farewell to her classmates. "But we will have to wait so very long. Everything goes slowly but this will go at the speed of a tortoise."[30]

How are we to understand these intimate details in Blanche Bendahan's portrayal of Tetouan? Were they gleaned from her childhood visits and those she made as an adult when writing *Mazaltob*? Did she turn to scholarly or auto-ethnographic accounts? Undoubtedly. Yet an additional, even more compelling, source lies in the epistolary tradition of the teachers in the Alliance Israélite Universelle schools. Their letters, especially those written from Tetouan during the years in which the novel takes place and housed in the Paris archives of the AIU, might have offered Blanche Bendahan a treasure trove of firsthand accounts.

A tragic accident, for example, occurs in the novel on the Muslim holiday of 'Id al Kabir (which honors Ibrahim's willingness to sacrifice his son Ismail) when Mazaltob's little brother is run over by an Arab horseman. Blanche could well have imagined such an incident, for no record exists in any published historical account. Yet a letter from Tetouan to Paris in April 1893 provides vivid details of a twelve-year-old Jewish boy accidentally trampled to death by a young Arab on the first day of the fast of Ramadan.[31] The account, so powerful in the telling, bears striking similarity to that found in *Mazaltob*.[32] So much so that one can easily imagine Blanche sitting in the *bibliothèque* of the Alliance, removing the rusting straight pins from its carefully preserved correspondence.

Blanche's inscription in the copy of the novel she presented to the Alliance—"To the Alliance I give this book in homage"—suggests that she shared Mazaltob's gratitude to this organization. Yet as so often is the case with Blanche Bendahan, affection and respect do not preclude critical assessment. And thus, we learn early on that Mazaltob's "nostalgia for France" was ironically for a country she would never know.

Blanche may well have found inspiration for the persona of Mazaltob in Hassiba Coriat, a young Alliance teacher. In the summer of 1892, having spent four years in Paris at a normal school, Hassiba returned home to Tetouan to assist the Director of the Alliance girls' school. Responsible for only two classes, she had time to continue with her studies, even to write thoughtful essays on the historical significance of the eighteenth century, the profession of teaching, and the position of women. In this last essay, after providing literary, religious, and political examples from

Biblical times to the present, Hassiba presented the reader with a radical model—that of a woman choosing any profession, "whether teacher, couturier, doctor, merchant or even lawyer."[33]

Hassiba wrote one final essay—on suffering and those who succumbed—before accepting a marriage proposal from Jacob Pariente. He had returned from Caracas a wealthy man, willing and able to support Hassiba's large family. (Like our protagonist Mazaltob, Hassiba had nine brothers and sisters.) He also agreed to pay the Alliance for the six years Hassiba had yet to serve (as in the métropole ten years were required) for he believed that a wife should not work after marriage.

We know little more of Hassiba Coriat after she married and departed Tetouan for Venezuela, other than that she was very beautiful—this from an interview with her niece—and beloved by students and teachers alike.[34] Had Blanche met Hassiba when in Tetouan during one of her family visits? Perhaps. She would certainly have learned of Hassiba's marriage and departure for the new world, since Blanche's paternal grandmother was a member of Hassiba's Coriat family.

Some of the themes in *Mazaltob*, however, have less resonance in turn-of-the-century Tetouan than in the conflict-ridden atmosphere of Oran. By her weaving them into the tale, Tetouan also became for Blanche a stand-in for her birthplace and residence.[35] The lure of westernization, for example, the all-too-easy abandonment of tradition, and the crass imitation of colonial hubris may have reflected the atmosphere in Tetouan, but also, and more pointedly, they speak to Blanche Bendahan's Algeria.

Discussions among Mazaltob's family and friends around the differences between Judaism and Christianity, or those decrying religious bigotry and the prevalence of antisemitism, have even less resonance in turn-of-the-century Tetouan.

"The people of Oran," Albert Camus complained in a 1939 essay, "have closed the window, they have walled themselves in, they have exorcised the landscape."[36] Camus had in mind the "ugly buildings" recently erected in Oran, many facing inward and away from the sea. But his is also a fitting metaphor for the dissonance Blanche experienced between Oran's natural beauty and cosmopolitan charm—which she extolled even in her later years of exile—and its politically charged, often antisemitic, climate.

Blanche had spent her youth in a France rent asunder by the infamous

Dreyfus Affair, when a young Jewish Captain, unanimously convicted of treason, was subject to public military degradation and imprisoned on Devil's Island. In Alfred Dreyfus's presumed guilt, France's republic stood accused along with its emancipation of the Jews. Antisemitism remained an undercurrent throughout Algeria—the infamous antisemite Edmond Drumont had launched his political career there—even after the exoneration of Dreyfus in 1906. It was stoked by French settlers' hostility to the Crémieux Decree which, by granting the majority of Algeria's Jews French citizenship, also made possible their outvoting the settlers. An antisemitic party emerged in Oran in 1921, and before long swastikas were to be found throughout the country.

With this political climate in mind, Blanche was no doubt deliberatively provocative when she chose to dedicate her "Jewish novel" to her Catholic stepmother, Marie Hortense Ginoux. She is also unexpectedly autobiographical, for a careful reader of *Mazaltob* cannot fail to notice the similarities between Blanche's stepmother and Mazaltob's beloved voice teacher Madame Gérard, the wife of the French consul, or Blanche's own father and Mazaltob's cosmopolitan Uncle Salomon, who traveled widely and thought broadly, yet never abandoned his beloved Tetouan and his cherished faith.

And then, of course, there is Blanche Bendahan herself. She, too, has a counterpart in the novel. Mazaltob's childhood friend and beloved soulmate is Jean, the nephew and adopted "son" of Doctor Bralakoff. Jean, like Blanche, has a Christian and a Jewish parent, only in Jean's case his mother is Jewish and his father a Christian. And like Blanche, Jean is delicate, fair-haired, a poet, and an advocate for women's education. Neither Christian nor Jewish, his is a cosmic God who "soars over vengeance and hatred."[37] That Blanche Bendahan's middle name is Jeanne only confirms their interconnectedness.

But perhaps most telling of all is Jean's ardent request that Mazaltob accompany him to France. Mazaltob's initial response to Jean, and thus Blanche Bendahan's response to herself as well, echoes the Greek poet C.P. Cavafy's plaintive farewell to the Alexandria of his birth: "As if long prepared for this, as if courageous, bid her farewell."[38] Mazaltob, however, a "woman of Tetouan," could not bid adieu to her place of birth. Neither could Blanche Bendahan, who sought instead to bridge her disparate worlds. Nevertheless, in the language of a colonialist culture, she was drawn to revisiting this farewell—as poet, orientalist, feminist, and proud member of Tetouan's extended Sephardi community.

"We often fabricate our views and our prejudices en masse," Doctor Bralakoff's Ashkenazic daughter-in-law Léa explains. "We are like captains who maneuver their boats the same way regardless of the weather. As for all that belongs to the past, it is little different, for when we say: 'this is foolish,' perhaps it is we who are judging foolishly.'"[39] Léa's warning—addressed both to Jean and to us as readers—speaks to the perils of succumbing to a presumptuous vision of the past and a prejudiced understanding of the present. It resonates throughout Blanche Bendahan's novel, as does her determination to shed light, with humor and miraculous irony, on the struggles of her time.

Note on Translation

It is a truism that the challenges of translation are specific to each work. As a novel deeply enmeshed in four different linguistic and cultural universes—the Judeo-Spanish, the French, the Arabic, and the Hebrew—*Mazaltob* presented its own set of difficulties. It is in many ways already a work of translation in the original French, for it proposed to bring to a French audience a culture it scarcely knew—the Sephardi world from Tetouan specifically, and Sephardism in general.

For the French-to-English translators, the challenges posed by *Mazaltob* were manifold. We had to preserve Bendahan's rich borrowings from those other languages, as she mixed them with her French text, to yield the *métissage* Bendahan clearly intended. One must read *Mazaltob* as a tapestry, a patchwork of sorts, a reflection of the multilayered universe of the Sephardim at the crossroads of cultures. *Mazaltob* abounds in parentheses, appositions, footnotes, italics, and em dashes. At a time, the 1920s, when the expansion of the French colonial empire of the previous century was entrenched, scores of exotic novels introduced readers to newly discovered and faraway locales. Bendahan's novel had a clear didactic purpose, intended as it must have been for a non-Jewish readership.

As translators, we have at times followed Bendahan's cues, choosing like her to retrieve the original source. Mazaltob's sister is Précieuse in the novel, a translation of Preciada—a common name in Judeo-Spanish. Why not use the English Precious? Or why not keep Précieuse? We decided instead to restore her name to the more authentic Preciada, and a similar choice was made for Mazaltob's surname. In the original French text, Bendahan chose to gallicize it, changing it to Massiah, while we stayed true to the Tetouani patronym: Macías. Our own text became, ironically, the translation of a translation.

At the same time, *Mazaltob* cannot solely be read as a work of ethnography. Seeking not to burden the reader, foreign words in our rendering were italicized and translated once, after which they appear in roman

Note on Translation

characters. Bendahan's novel set out to delight as much as to instruct. This has impelled us, when possible, to lighten the load of explanatory apparatus by placing it at the end of the novel. Footnotes—both author's and editors'—appear seriatim, the latter in square brackets. We hoped in this manner to grant readers the liberty to conduct their own explorations.

Mazaltob

BLANCHE BENDAHAN

To Madame Marie Ginoux,
A Catholic,
Who So Tenderly Guided My Childhood,
I dedicate
This Jewish Novel

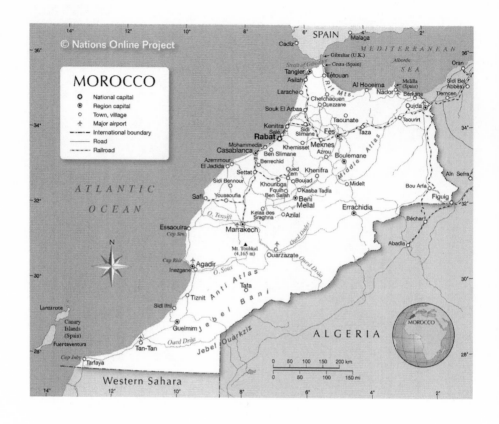

Political Map of Morocco. Nations Online Project

Chapter 1

She is a ravishing little girl with eyes bigger than her mouth, like those one finds in young people pictured in chromolithographs.

Her tresses are as dark as those of Shulamit. But therein ends the resemblance with King Solomon's beloved, for this beautiful little girl isn't black, but rather extraordinarily white, so white that not a trace of rose tints her cheeks.

For the beautiful little girl has never played in a park with water fountains, bowling greens, and statues, as one finds in large cities.

She has neither played in one of those gardens of the French provinces whose manicured lawns are adorned with a gazing ball.

Nor has she played on a farmyard, when the smell of cut hay overwhelms that of dung, and small chicks like fuzzy yellow balls chirp as they chase each other.

The beautiful young girl has never played at all.

But once or twice during the ten years of her life, as she stood near the city's gates, she admired the countryside from afar. She saw the trees. She saw the brooks. She saw the flowers . . .

Just enough for her soul to be filled with regrets.

The beautiful little girl, who at home spoke only an archaic Spanish known as *ladino*,[1] has studied the language of Voltaire at the school of the Alliance. She has also studied French history and geography. She knows by heart a few passages from the works of our great poets. Just enough to feel nostalgic about a country she will probably never know and will always love as much as if it were her own.

*   *   *

The beautiful little girl, who is the fifth of eight children, was born in Tetouan in the Jewish quarter.

She never sees her mother elegantly dressed until Friday's deep cleaning is complete, when dusk lights the stars and instantly kindles in each room the candles for the Sabbath.

The floors have been scrubbed again and again. The aromas of the simmering *albondigas*² fill the entire household.

The beautiful little girl will be an accomplished woman.

Early on we taught her to respect all that pertains to religion. When one of her younger brothers drops a prayer book, she screams, as per tradition: "The head!"³ which is short for: "May your head drop sooner than a sacred book!"

But she has never given much thought to the cruel meaning of her words.

The beautiful little girl is clever. When we send her out to buy "white" she goes to the coalman. Why? Because she knows full well that by giving the thing its real name, the "black" that is the color of mourning, she would risk drawing the attention to her family of *el huerco*, the angel of death.

The beautiful little girl has a kind heart.

Every day, on her way back from school, after doing her homework, after studying her lessons, after putting her baby brother to sleep, after bathing her sister and combing her hair, she still finds time to run errands for her invalid grandmother.

And the old lady, moved by such kindness, bestows blessings on her in the manner of Tetouan: "Oh Mazaltob,⁴ my light, your name means: good luck. I wish upon you one hundred years of happiness. That you may marry. That you may give birth to boys. That your home may be filled with circumcisions and communions!...Oh Mazaltob, picture of joy, clear diamond, your name and your beauty will bring you luck."

* * *

Baudelaire dreamt of a mineral landscape like this. Everywhere, gray stone, strangling the horizon.

Passageways like narrow corridors. The tiniest windows with screens made of a fine wire netting that would never allow for a branch or a flower to find its way in. On the ground, pressed against each other like rows of herrings from the Nordic seas, the small pointy pavements cannot exhale a single blade of green grass.

4

Mazaltob

The Judería[5]—or Jewish quarter—knows nothing about the seasons.

Only the heat and cold, as well as the blue sky streaming narrowly along the ridges of the houses above them, enable its inhabitants to tell winter from summer.

Misbehaving, an old building once in a while straddles the street, and while noises become crisper under its canopy, the scents of clover and melted honey linger there more languidly. Anonymous for the most part, unaware of the recesses and respite plazas might offer, one corridorlike alley succeeds another.

Their lime mixed in with pigments of color, the walls of one *calleja*, or lane, turn pink, while those of another turn blue. These differences in shade serve as points of reference for the tourist who wanders through this labyrinth of doors, nail-studded like a soldier's boots. Here and there, the same box-like grocery shop, drugstore, or haberdashery recurs like a leitmotif, always without a distinguishing sign.

* * *

On that day, caught between the vise-like walls, the sky seems to flow like a clear blue stream. And on that fine day, as Mazaltob's mother and her two youngest siblings stay home, on that very fine day, with each donkey carrying a grown-up or two children, Mazaltob goes with her family to Kitane for the first time ever.

Orange-picking is about to begin.

* * *

Mazaltob marvels: so much sky at once, what a godsend!

And all this while barely raising her head as she does in her bleak neighborhood. She finds the clouds amusing. They resemble those snowy egg whites beaten stiff which her mother slips inside the oven to bake meringues.

Does the ground burn the legs of such a nervous sparrow?...

Like a prisoner suddenly set free, the child, with her eyes, is feasting on all that space.

She runs to the right. She runs to the left. Each one of her footsteps is a kiss for the blooming earth.

Weary at last, she sits on the grass where light scatters like shards of

5

the morning dew. A delicate breeze disperses the peppery fragrance of orange trees.

Mazaltob shuts her eyes, opens her nostrils, and drinks in the fresh air: for the first time, she realizes she is breathing.

On the other side there is bustling about, as the ship which will carry Kitane's famous oranges to England is already docked at the Bay of Rio Martine, Tetouan's natural seaport.

Beneath the swift hands of the Arabs stripping them, the small trees shudder and whisper. David Macías[6] is Mazaltob's father and the seller of oranges, and Pinhas Barchilon is the harvest's buyer. Each has a branch of quince tree and a well-sharpened knife in hand.

Ishoa, the youngest of the boys, counts the fruits out loud as they are tossed into baskets.

Every time Eliayu, the eldest, proclaims a thousand has been reached, each man cuts a notch on their respective branches.

Later, the total amount will be as easy to determine. It will go unchallenged.

* * *

"Where do you come from, face of light?" Doctor Bralakoff strokes Mazaltob's cheek.

Born at the end of the world—in Russia—the doctor is an Askhkenazi Jew.

This difference, which makes him a *forastero*, meaning a stranger, does not prevent the Sephardim[7] of Tetouan from loving him, thus breaking for once with their tradition of hostility.

For isn't he as much a *haham*[8] as Rabbi Isaac Nahon and Rabbi Isaac Bengualid[9] whose graves are greatly honored?

Hasn't he healed numerous sons of Israel who were ripe for the eternal rest of the great *me'ara?*[10]

May he be healthy...

Although he has only been a father once in his life, Doctor Bralakoff has two sons.

The second one is his nephew. In his veins, the Christian blood of a Frenchman mingles with the blood of the Bralakoffs. Illness and pogroms made him an orphan, and since then the kind doctor loves him as much as Serge, the son he had with his wife, who is now resting—resting in peace.

"Where do you come from, Mazaltob...? How beautiful you are! We've never seen her flushed like this, Jean, have we?"

Jean, the Christian—he wasn't circumcised, the poor thing!—responds with a nod of his blonde head.

"Joy renders her mute," explains old Macías who appears at that moment. "We took her to Kitane where she ran wild all day."

"For God's sake, I understand that: a new broom sweeps clean."[11]

Mazaltob gazes at Jean. Is flesh really covering his astonishingly white and pink face? What are such blue eyes made of?...

How lovely is his hair whose color resembles the gold of the bracelets worn by women on their arms on the holy day of the Sabbath!...

And Jean gazes at Mazaltob, that beautiful little girl happiness renders more beautiful, more beautiful even than ever.

> "I had a crush one night
> And the moon duped me.
> I thought she was beautiful
> But she was uglier than I."

Thus sings Ishoa, the youngest.

Mazaltob leafs through a French almanac.

These beautiful Parisian ladies are so funny, with their slender doll's waists, gigot sleeves, and funnel skirts!

There the married women are often more attractive than the single girls because they don't need to hide their hair under the traditional headscarf.

And Mazaltob sadly strokes her brown tresses.

How long will her family let her keep them? Five years...? Six years...? The girls from Tetouan must all marry young.

Mazaltob leafs through the almanac.

Here is the stage of a theater with magical dancers. Here an elegant Amazon rides a galloping horse. And there a crowd applauds a singer with swooning eyes.

But who kneads the daily bread? Who makes the almond cakes...?
Who distills the anisette? Who prepares the orange blossom jam?

Who makes the palm tree brooms...?

Who runs the household of these pretty ladies who seem to exist only to be admired, and who, astonishingly, go out without their husband?

The strange life of the *goyim* from the big city is quite intriguing to Mazaltob.

*   *   *

Thank God—may His name be praised!—there are more boys than girls in the Macías family. Mazaltob has indeed only two sisters. At eighteen, one of them is already old and the other is nearly still a baby.

The name of the older one is Preciada.

Unfortunately, our Preciada has a face long as the fast of Yom Kippur, eyes like shrunken buttonholes, and the hair of a black woman which will likely benefit from disappearing under the matrimonial headscarf.

The pallor of the sunless Judería does nothing for her darker skin tone. Besides, her cheeks are covered with pimples.

"Marriage will cure that," the elderly ladies say.

The slightest cold weather swells with blisters her already thick fingers. Marriage will also cure that.

Preciada is grumpy because of her stomach ailments.

Marriage will cure both her stomach and her grumpiness.

Hence the elder Miss Macías dreams ceaselessly of her future nuptials.

But alas, in these first months of the year 1900, she saw the end of her eighteenth year and the beginning of her sorrows.

"Isn't such a long wait ridiculous...? The sheets from her *ajuar*[12] have all yellowed. What! Will she never be able to immerse herself in the ritual bath of Tebilah where young girls must purify themselves on the eve of their marriage?

Will she never know the glory of giving birth? Wo...Wo...Wo...[13] God forbid!"

*   *   *

Mazaltob can't solve a math problem and is so unnerved that her eyes fill up with tears. She will no doubt lose first place in school.

"Ishoa, please, explain to me..."

"No, girls don't need to learn so much arithmetic..."

"What about you, Jacob...? Will you...?"

"No, I am going to Znoga."[14]

Burying her head in her hands, Mazaltob now starts sobbing...Then she hears:

"You must simply cross-multiply, subtract, then divide."

The girl's wet eyes meet the light face of Jean the Christian.

He is commenting on the calculations that his diligent pen is jotting down on a piece of paper. Mazaltob is able to understand.

"How nice you are...thank you...thank you..."

"Don't thank me, pretty girl. To see you cry burns my eyes."

Chapter 2

Mazaltob, who is now past thirteen, has become a young woman.

On that occasion, she had to dip her index finger in a honey pot in front of her mother.

When she pulled it out, the old maid started to shrill joyfully, her guttural *bargouelas* endlessly piercing the air in the patio...[1]

Mazaltob may now marry. Her womb is ripe for childbearing. May the God of Abraham give her sons...!

You...You...You...!

* * *

Through the parsimonious netting of the window an old Spanish ballad sneaks in.

> *"Listen, Mister soldier,*
> *If from the battle you have come..."*
> *"Yes, Madam, 'tis from the battle indeed,*
> *The battle of the Englishman."*
> *"If once, perchance,*
> *My husband you have come upon..."*
> *"Your husband I do not know*
> *And have not the faintest inkling who he is."*[2]

"Oh the delightful voice...! Do you know who is singing, young man?"

"It is my sister, Madam."

"Is that so? And what is her name?"

"Mazaltob Macías."

"Mazaltob...the one who is so beautiful?"

"Yes."

Mazaltob

"That man you spoke of
Perished more than thirty days past
And before he died, he asked
That I wed you."
"Shush, shush, my lord
Do not speak so daringly.
Seven years I have waited,
And seven more years I shall wait…"

"Mister Macías, would you please ask your mother whether she would care to greet the wife of the French consul, Madame Gérard?"

"Fourteen years have ended,
*   and if he still has not returned,*
A nun I shall become,
A nun like Saint Clare,
A nun like Doña Inès."

"Madam, my mother awaits you."

∗ ∗ ∗

It's an unprecedented, an extraordinary event.

From the first morning prayer, or Tefilah, until Arbit, the evening one, talk is all everyone in the Judería does:

Mazaltob, "the one from" father Macías the chubby, is taking voice lessons with the French consul's wife.

A swell lady, that Madame Gérard, a very swell lady, but a bit fussy—likely because the poor woman never had a child of her own…!

To waste time teaching a young girl to sing, what a strange occurrence…!

And operas at that? When their Judeo-Spanish ancestors had brought to Tetouan ballads from Castilla like "The City of Toledo" and "The Moorish Queen Xerifa"? And what about the joyous wedding piyyutim…?

As though she weren't *flamenga* enough,[3] that Mazaltob, in her way of speaking without moving her hands!

We'd better teach her how to cook *adafina*,[4] the delicious dish we feast upon on Saturdays.

So, when Mazaltob returns from her twice-weekly lessons, everyone in the Judería is out on their doorsteps.

And the neck of the crimson-faced adolescent sinks beneath her shoulders. O, shame on her! She has dared something no one else ever did!

* * *

"Farewell, Uncle Salomon, till tomorrow. I must get back home early. Mother is feeling a bit unwell, so I will have to knead dough to make bread myself. I must also bake bread for almsgiving, since today is Thursday."[5]

"Good, good, young lady. May the light illuminate your path...! And blessed be our holy Tetouan community which never let a son of Israel go unnourished!"

"Could such a thing happen elsewhere, Uncle?"

Uncle Salomon is well traveled. He appeared by turns in the census of London, Berlin, Paris, Florence, and New York.

Like many of his brethren, he has decided in old age to return home. For is it not terrible to die far from the land of your forebears...?

Uncle Salomon gazes at Mazaltob: What a sweet child! Naïve and beautiful in equal measure!

He then begins talking.

He speaks of the wretched winters of the Northern countries, their gray rivers, and their grand bridges. Under their somber arches shelter shivering men, women, and sometimes children, pangs of hunger contracting their empty stomach.

He speaks of the icy nights when pitiful shadows wander.

He speaks of the tragic "splashes" of bodies shrouded only in water.

He speaks of the December mornings when, stiffened by death, an old grandfather with a frosty beard is tossed on the slabs of a morgue.

He speaks of the noose which hangs from the ceiling beams of a hovel.

He speaks of the small deadly stoves, their smoke ever consoling those who received neither bread, nor synagogue alms, nor the pious queries of the rabbi during the *nedaba*.[6]

O Mazaltob, o delicate face, o queen! Remember that all Jews are brothers and we have no right, do you hear, *no right at all*, to forget those among us in need.

May he choke, he who can eat and digest and not think about misfortune...!

O Mazaltob, notwithstanding the jealous hatred of nations, solidarity alone will enable the descendants of Jacob to reach the end of time...!

* * *

An old lady had come to the house of David Macías to propose a husband for Preciada.

But Mazaltob's father began screaming loudly when he heard that his would-be son-in-law was a cobbler. What? To give his daughter to a *taraf*, as a cobbler is known among ordinary people.

He hasn't yet gone mad!

Infuriated, he starts railing against the old lady:

"*Malograda*,[7] what are you thinking of...! Do you know we come from a noble and ancient family? Do you know neither my father nor my grandfather or even great-grandfather ever once worked with his hands?

"As for me, these hard times have impelled me to work in the orange trade, but I fortunately have under my orders a dozen Arabs, who are not unlike those Hebrew slaves we used to call *abadim*.[8]

"Go tell your taraf of doom to propose to the daughter of a cooper or a tinker.

"With God's help—praised be His name!—Preciada will marry into a good family."

Drawn by the shouting, the rest of the family consents to the master's words in respectful silence. Mazaltob is quiet, too... but she is thinking.

She has read several French novels where kings marry shepherdesses and shepherds marry queens... Perhaps Preciada would be happy with this cobbler, for he is said to be a man of principles.

But isn't a father's judgment infallible...?

* * *

"Jean, you are neither a Christian nor a Jew...Will you remain that way forever?"

"I do not know, Mazaltob."

"How so . . . ?"

"Father wishes I not decide until twenty-one."

"O! Surely you will not hesitate . . . ! Isn't our religion the most beautiful of all?"

"There is no religion I find beautiful."

"Is that true? Aren't you proud of being Jewish?"

"No."

"What if I asked you to believe in the God of Abraham, to be one of ours at last, would you say yes . . . ? I would be so glad to do a Mitzvah."[9]

Sitting on a low chair, Mazaltob lifts her eyes toward Jean.

Her extraordinary endless lashes flutter. The apples of her magnificent eyes float like black velvet islands on a misty oval pond.

Her supple lips, as if held between brackets, reach for a smile. Her nascent breasts quiver.

And Jean, shaken at the very core of his eighteen years, answers: "Yes . . . no . . . maybe . . . Mazaltob."

Chapter 3

Mazaltob has just turned sixteen and everyone from Larache to Melilla talks about her marvelous face.

She may not be very tall, but her curves, at once shapely and slender, make it hard to wish for anything more perfect.

One false note only in such harmony: her hands, albeit slim and very white, are a bit chapped from doing housework.

For since her father's bankruptcy, Mazaltob has had few distractions.

Child number nine was recently born to the family—thank God it's a boy!—and everyone thinks Mrs. Macías, who is only thirty-seven, will still have many more. Isn't it a blessing from heaven to bring forth many children?

Thus far, however, heaven seems rather indifferent to Mazaltob's parents, for their progeny increases in a manner inversely proportional to their fortune: the last sailboat carrying oranges from Kitane sank. A house owned by the Macíases in the Judería collapsed.

And old father Macías no longer has his health.

Preciada had the good fortune to wed when the family was still prosperous, and her lavish trousseau was greatly admired by the mother and the sisters of her fiancé.

But alas, she has now been married for two years, and her flesh has still not borne a child. And the eldest of the Macíases, like in the old days, has a reason to complain:

"Who has given me the evil eye...? Is it not laughable to be barren for so long...? Will I ever listen to the *you-yous* of circumcisions in my own home...? Wo...Wo...Wo...God forbid...!"

*　*　*

Mazaltob, who is too busy at home, had to stop taking voice lessons.

She nonetheless each Saturday pays a visit to her guardian, Madame

Gérard. After a maternal kiss from her, they hurry off to the piano where the passionate words and sounds miraculously arise again.

Mazaltob has learned to control the rare timbre of her lovely contralto voice, but she gives an expressiveness to the musical phrase, which comes not from technique, but rather her soul.

Mazaltob sings and the sky seems higher. Vast expanses of green materialize in place of the stifling Judería.

Through the foliage, young girls dressed in white suddenly appear dancing and holding hands. Mazaltob sings. She then joins the next round of dancers.

How light she feels...! What a sweet exhilaration...! The morning bursts with chattering birds and sparkles everywhere with myriad droplets of dew.

Mazaltob sings. A blonde creature, beautiful as an angel, sits at her feet. A blonde creature, with crystal blue eyes.

Mazaltob sings. Mazaltob escapes far from the bleak bondages of her life. Mazaltob sings. Mazaltob is euphoric.

But Madame Gérard, who thinks of the young woman's future, wonders: "Have I made a mistake?"

For her books have already opened up new horizons for Mazaltob beyond the narrow Judería. And yet, like her sisters, she remains bound by the strict law of Moses.

And like all the other Jewish women, she will no doubt submit to her destiny—to increase Israel's posterity and fulfill the wishes of the God of Abraham.

All to ensure that the greatest number of praises may be sung to glorify Adonaï our God. Mazaltob worries only about the small insignificant things in life such as producing perfect preserves in her kitchen or obtaining the right shade of white on the patio's walls.

Mazaltob is just another Jewish girl. But this is only an appearance, for Mazaltob has also had a taste of the dream...

The DREAM...!

She knows there is a thing called love. It's a kind of love unknown in the Judería—the love, for instance, Tristan feels for Isolde and Romeo for Juliet.

She knows that in some countries—far, far from Tetouan—men and women who worship each other would rather die than be apart.

In some countries—far, far from Tetouan—attractive young men and women get drunk on love in the course of magical full-moon nights. She knows, too, that in some countries, love either of the forbidden kind or the other one, is the ultimate purpose of life.

But isn't that far, very far, from Tetouan?

* * *

It's *noche sabbat*, the Eve of Shabbat.

At the end of the service, it is customary to visit the elderly. Much like ancient Rome, Tetouan, ever behind the times, has great respect for its elders.

This is why there is a big crowd at the house of Yomtob Chocron and his wife.

The old patriarch and his wife—who sits arched like an odd fairy Carabosse,[1] her hair wrapped in a scarf embroidered in gold—put on airs as they hold court outside on their patio.

Sons, daughters, sons-in-law, daughters-in-law, and grandchildren, kissing their hand, all wish them "Peace on the Sabbath" and sit next to them. Visitors, overflowing from everywhere, stretch all the way to the kitchen's entrance.

The news of the week is traded from ear to ear, and as in all other civilized countries, there is gossip, too.

"The Levys have bought a large house in the Judería"

"Is that so...? How fast they have grown!"

"Ruben Isso still has not proposed to Luna Attias."

"Not surprising. Always on the fence, that one."

"Excuse me, it's rather Luna's father who does not care for Ruben as his son-in-law."

"Nonsense...! He is eager to hand him his daughter with seven hands!"[2]

"I know what it's all about: Luna, who is only fifteen, is still a child...!"

"She should hurry to be of marriageable age. Ruben, who is thirty-seven already, is eager to start a family."

"Sarah, from Mimoun, the redhead, is three-months pregnant."

"Really? After seven years of marriage?"

"It's the truth. I swear on *your* life."[3]

"Makhlouf, from Moïse, is going to America."

"Why would he do that? Why? He has money."

"The book of Why has too many pages."

"It was Saftaray yesterday at the Carcienteses' house."

"They must be thrilled they finally married off that ugly daughter of theirs."

"She has a great many qualities...At least that's what her mother says."

"For God's sake! One of our proverbs says it: 'Who would praise the bride more than her miserable mother?'"

"The Barchilons now have six entrance lights to their home."

"How else could they flaunt their newly acquired piles of gold?"

"You know what we say of parvenus: '*Patas que nunca vieron saraouel.*'"[4]

"That's because no one ever told them 'Let the light illuminate your life.'"

Everyone laughs: Moïsito is such a witty child!

But only a moment later, tittle-tattle and gossip resume:

"Have you seen Mazaltob Macías lately?"

"Yes. She is a diamond in the rough. A beauty like Sol Hatchuel, our saintly martyr."[5]

"Do you really find her that pretty? She is so white she scares me," says a dark-skinned woman.

"Nonsense! We Jews are afraid only of black, which is the color for mourning."

"She is in any case a bit eccentric."

"That's true. One can barely hear her when she speaks."

"*Mi bueno*, in Europe, no one talks loudly."

"It's different when she sings. I was passing by the French consulate once and I asked myself who could be giving birth."

"All of you are nothing but a jealous bunch...!"

"Jealous...? Not at all. I swear on my father."[6]

"Jealous...? Jealous of what...? She has no money."

"You are envious of her beauty."

"Not in the slightest. Doesn't the proverb say: *La suerte de la fea, la bonita la desea?*"[7]

Mazaltob

"What's all this chatter...?!" Uncle Salomon asks as he comes in. "I cannot hear you when you speak all at once, you wicked tongues! But listen to me: whether you like it or not, whether you wish her well or not, Mazaltob, the finest flower of Israel, will fulfill the destiny promised in her name one day."

* * *

"I have been here nearly a month, and Mazaltob is all I hear about. I wish to meet her now."

"I can easily introduce you to her family. As for Mazaltob..."

"Is she blonde or brunette?"

"Her eyes and her hair are brown, but her skin is that of a blonde."

"That type of beauty is rather common in Argentina."

"Perhaps... But her eyes are unrivaled. One look from them would breathe life back to the dying."

"What enthusiasm! Why not ask yourself for her hand in marriage?"

"I am not yet twenty. I have three sisters to marry off. And I must go abroad to earn a good living."

"In the event I would fancy her, I may join the ranks of her suitors. How old is this gem?"

"She is sixteen."

"And I am close to forty. But these May-December marriages are far from unusual around here."

"And you are rich..."

"That's a sure thing."

"Well, cousin, you are welcome to come to the Macías house tomorrow if you'd like."

"Certainly, Abraham," says José.

* * *

> *"A man with a crush*
> *On a theater actress*
> *Is like one who is hungry*
> *And is fed baking soda"*

...hums José Jalfon while getting dressed.

19

Thanks to his wealth, he's known plenty of actresses. He's also known plenty of sophisticated women, for he is proud to have sown his wild oats in Buenos Aires.

But as he nears forty now, he knows it is time to button up his pants and get hitched.

There, in the other world (that's what he calls the new continent), there is no shortage of pretty ladies. Yes, but unlike several other countries, there are lots of men and few women—which means greater competition.

And Jewish families with eligible daughters are much harder "to spot" in the big city.

Even harder, how would he learn about the background and the morality of these families who have been in America for only a few years or barely a generation?

That's why the majority of Sephardi Jews living in Argentina, Brazil, or Venezuela take a trip back home as soon as their heart—or reason—calls for them to start a family.

They make their way first to Tetouan, a repository of exportable damsels, and in the unlikely event they cannot find one to suit their taste, the scope of their search expands to the region that extends from Tangier to Melilla.

No one in Spanish Morocco likes to see their maidens grow old. And because it often takes years in America to increase capital for those who started penniless, most aspiring husbands who return to Tetouan are greying at the temples.

In view of the wealth and of the patrician origins of such suitors, Tetouani fathers, flattered, give their youngest daughters to them with seven hands. The girls who are "north of twenty" and who remain in Tetouan are rather the exception.

* * *

On the large Transatlantic vessels carrying the newlyweds to the shores of Christopher Columbus, the goyim look at them and this is what they say to themselves:

"There goes father and daughter."

Never has one of these youths been reported to rebel against such a state of affairs. Everyone is so accustomed to these unions!

For is there anything to be done against heat, cold, illness, old age, or death...?

"Salomon, I may be the only one not agreeing with David. But it is folly to give Mazaltob, only sixteen, to this man."

"And why is that, Doctor...? I am older than my wife by twenty years, and it has in no way caused her to suffer."

"Have you ever asked her?"

"No. But I know that my mother was twenty years younger than my father and that one of my sisters is thirty years younger than her husband. I also know that a woman's beauty fades very fast and that a man must be able to look at a fresh face for as long as he can to not be tempted to seek another woman, as that is reproved by God."

"Poor women...!"

"Why do you feel sorry for them...? And furthermore, were they to experience a few disappointments, would motherhood not cause them to forget about them?"

"Motherhood...! It is true one does not marry in this country because a man of our liking is essential to us, or because we ache to love and to be loved. One marries here to procreate."

"Isn't that to obey the will of God and that of Nature?"

"Believe me, Bralakoff, your people and others attain the same goal by way of Poetry and Ideals. But here we have neither theater, nor concerts, nor balls, nor novels, nor poems to dupe us or act as smokescreens. Indeed, we act in a very frank way."

"Salomon, I see that despite your extensive travels you have remained Tetouani to the core. But you know as much as I do that there is a thing called love."

"Love? Is that the name you give that stupid folly which lasts a few days, a few months, and sometimes a few years...? What's all of that in the face of a saintly lifelong marriage? No, Bralakoff, no, my dear doctor, love does not exist. There is family and home."

* * *

"Ah! There you are, José! Come forth to kiss me, *mi bueno*. I have heard of your engagement to Mazaltob. The beauty of her face is unmatched."

21

"May it be for the best. *Que sea para bien.* May she give you many sons. And may I be sacrificed in lieu of you, oh my light!"

"Thank you, thank you, sister Nedjma.[8] May you stay healthy and may you live to one hundred."

"Thank you, *mi alma,* my soul. Please come to sweeten your mouth so that your life may be sweet, too. Here, help yourself to some of these candied eggplants..."

"But it is nearly noon... and that would cause me to lose my appetite for lunch."

"You are not going to refuse, are you?"

José acquiesces, resigned. He knows all too well it is always a good time in this land "to sweeten the mouth." He also knows that refusing a sweet is most indecorous, even if indigestion follows.

He suspects old Nedjma did not invite him merely to congratulate him. Indeed.

"You, my dear, are coming from America, so you'll be able to bring me news from my son. You must have seen him."

"Well, no... Buenos Aires is a large city..."

"Buenos Aires...? He is in Venezuela."

"Venezuela? Have you no idea of distances...?"

But old Nedjma, stubborn as she is ignorant, concludes, unimpressed:

"Maybe.... But you know, he is in America, too... It would not be surprising if you see him." Despite his serious airs, José barely contains his laughter. These old Jewish folks from Tetouan are priceless...!

* * *

"The beauty of her face is unmatched," said old Nedjma speaking of Mazaltob. José, too, thinks his fiancée is beautiful.

But his fiancée does not have that *je ne sais quoi,* what the French call *avoir du chien,* and the Spaniards, *salero.*

José, an Argentinian Tetouani, loves women who are cheerful, mischievous, and have a flirty gaiety to them.

Instead, Mazaltob opens her mouth only to answer questions. Is it because she is shy? Or stupid?

Whatever the reason, the betrothal period is anything but amusing— not a moment for them to be together alone. No chance to steal the smallest kiss. Always a chaperone from the family keeping watch on the future couple . . .

As is directed by Tetouani tradition.

"Ah . . . ! When will I be able to leave this bevy of old-fashioned dinosaurs behind?" wonders José, thinking of Argentina's free-wheeling ways.

For he hardly intends to settle in Tetouan, where everything is narrow: the streets, the prejudices, and the interpretation of the Holy Law.

"Indeed, everything is narrow here," Uncle Salomon once said. Everything . . . except the heart.

* * *

"Mazaltob, would you like to move to Argentina?"

After pondering the question, Mazaltob replies to José: "I would rather go to France."

"France . . . ? Why France?"

"I love France."

"But why do you love it?"

"Why . . . ? First because I feel grateful. Had it not been for France, I could neither read nor write. I probably would know nothing of history, geography, or literature . . ."

". . . of France. That famous school of the Alliance Israélite Universelle from Paris however has neglected to instruct you in the history, the geography, and the literature of other nations—in particular Spain, whose language you speak."

"Shame on Spain who did not think it fit to educate its Jews . . . ! After Jerusalem, France is the name that remains etched in my heart."

* * *

It is unusual that Mazaltob utters more than ten consecutive words, so this causes José to think for a while.

He was taken to Argentina at the age of six and only returned when he reached maturity. Hence he knows so little of his native city.

That love Sephardi Jews from Morocco feel for France, that respect those "Spaniards without a homeland" have for that great liberal nation,[9] is all due to the work of the Alliance Israélite Universelle.[10]

Thanks to that organization, founded in Paris in 1860, and to their network of schools throughout Morocco, the first of which opened in Tetouan in 1862—and thanks, finally, to a thirst for knowledge which characterizes the Jewish race—France has acquired a powerful spiritual colony among the descendants of Old Castille.

"Is that spiritual colony so powerful?" wonders José.

How could we doubt it . . . ? Aren't the territories conquered by France particularly attractive to young Jews who are of age to leave Tetouan, where they have no prospects?

And later they even choose to settle in France, a country of which they become citizens, generously spilling their very own blood for it, as the war of 1870 has proven!

Why doesn't South America, whose language is native to them, hold the same prestige? Because they are ignorant of its past.

Ah! A country's past . . . ! That amalgam of heroism and turpitudes, of miseries and glory, of perpetual suffering and struggles for an ideal . . . ! Isn't to learn also to understand?

And José thinks:

"It is a remarkable thing that the descendants of those Jews who spoke the archaic Spanish of ancient Castille should have such reverence for France and should direct their grateful eyes towards her."[11]

O land of Joan of Arc, how many unknown hearts belong thoroughly to you . . . !

* * *

The secret reign of France causes José to feel out of place in his native country.

Indeed, the basic French spoken in Buenos Aires will not enable him to read the novels of Balzac or of Victor Hugo in the original—as Mazaltob so easily does.

He thought he could subjugate that young Jewish girl; not only is she more cultivated than he, however, she also knows things he does not . . . !

And to not be admired is perilous, for he neither has charm nor youth. Will he effortlessly stay the master, as he used to think?

While José has remained a dutiful Jew despite living among the goyim, he does not elevate a woman more than he should.

Mazaltob

From the time he was pious, he remembers reciting each day in his morning prayers:

"May you be praised, O Lord, King of the Universe, that I was not born a woman."

Chapter 4

Toc. Toc. Toc. Toc.

The copper pestles clank inside their mortars.

Containers everywhere, each filled with flour, semolina, lemon zest, orange blossoms, or almonds.

Demijohns of oil and jars of honey everywhere!

Baskets with eggs, bowls overflowing with sugar, clovers, or cinnamon everywhere: The wedding celebrations will begin in eight days.

The mortars are tinkling:

Toc. Toc. Toc. Toc.

The Macías household is filled with a noisy bustling about. The children are gathered around an elderly maid who is rolling out cookie dough. Sitting in front of an earthen basin, she spins between her palms a stick whose tip is immersed in the pasty liquid. The eggs need to be adequately whipped, which will take a while, so the maid is humming an old Castilian melody:

"In the city of Toledo,
In the city of Aragon..."

Another woman watches over a copper cauldron in which an orange marmalade is boiling.

But the almond, oh, the famed almond! An essential ingredient for all Jewish confectionery, this traditional baking staple requires the care of many. Mustn't the almonds be peeled one by one and finely crushed in small batches?

And there are so many of them! It is as though a sailboat delivered an entire cargo of them to us! Crush, crush, crush!

Clank. Clank. Clank. Clank.

Flans, sweet in excess because they are made with coconut milk, are also being baked, but that's a rare indulgence. Jewish Tetouan has an aversion for creams made with butter—for creams should not be savored after eating meat, lest we transgress Jewish law.

Hands are busy crushing away:

Clank. Clank. Clank. Clank.

Beef tongue, which was cured with salt and saltpeter, has been ready for several days.

Extra help will be required to knead dough for bread: for all of that flour, several women will be needed!

We don't marry off a daughter to a millionaire every day...!

Everyone calls each other from room to room. All that din coming from the pestles makes it difficult to hear anything.

Toc. Toc. Toc. Toc.

The house's outer walls and the main façade were whitewashed two weeks ago. Curtains of white guipure lace, sparkling clean and properly starched, give the living room the fresh air of a child's bedroom.

Pestles jingle joyfully:

Toc. Toc. Toc. Toc.

The ceremony of *Bab al'Urs*, or the "gates of matrimony," which usually takes place on a Thursday, comes in eight days.

It's Mazaltob's Bab al 'Urs.

Mazaltob whose name is auspicious.

The pestle's brassy song steadily fills the air.

Toc. Toc. Toc. Toc.

* * *

"Madame, I have come to share with you the news of my imminent nuptials."

"So soon!" sighs Madame Gérard. "I thought your betrothal would last longer. My lovely Mazaltob, you are so young... But what does your young heart whisper in your ears?"

"Not much, Madame."

"How is that possible...? Could it be...perhaps...that you do not love your future husband?"

"I have neither like nor dislike for him."

"So why did you choose him, my dear?"

"Oh, madame! Our girls seldom choose their husbands. Their families usually do it."

The consul's wife gazes intensely at Mazaltob, who is speaking in a calm voice: what is hiding behind those magnificent eyes of hers...? Resignation? Indifference? Or pain?

But the eyes of the beautiful Jewish girl, which are customarily so expressive, allow no one to pierce their secret today.

"How about playing some music? Would you like that?"

"Oh, yes, Madame. One last time..."

"One last time...? But you'll come back, my child."

"Perhaps I will... But will I ever sing again?"

"Does your fiancé dislike music?"

"I do not know, Madame. I have not asked him."

"Really? But what does he think of your beautiful voice?"

"Nothing, Madame, for he has not heard me...

"...And I shall never sing for him,"[1] Mazaltob adds gravely.

In the *petit salon*'s penumbra, sounds now well up, burgeon, and flower. A voice suddenly darts forth, soars, and expands harmoniously, then, having reached its affecting climax, inflects, dulls, and calms down.

"It is the last time..." thinks Madame Gérard, her tender heart shrinking.

It is the last time...

Is that why Mazaltob's pitch is so poignant? And is that why a repressed sob cracks her voice on the last note?

* * *

A large lantern called *farol* in Spanish is hanging from the door of the Macías home to announce that a marriage is soon to be celebrated in the community.

On the chalk-white walls, friendly hands have written:

Happiness. Blissful marriage.

A tree with five branches, a flower bouquet, and a heart pierced with an arrow, all in blue ink, are likewise drawn on the walls.

Mazaltob

For today, on this Thursday of Bab al 'Urs, the festivities will commence.

Sponge cake, marzipan biscuits, *kaberzales* or gazelle horns, *marron chinos*, all are baked to perfection.

Candied eggplants—known as *méréhenitas*—are admirably flavored.

Orange blossom marmalade—or *azahar*—is neither too sticky nor too runny, and the angel's hair confiture, which has been prepared with candied strands of squash, turned out flawless. But Simi, who is the Macías's old maid, isn't happy: Messody and Sol—both are her rival cooks—have declared that the apple jelly came out too red.

Too red...! Still, it is superb. But it ought to be the color of white wine, as per tradition. And there is nothing more serious for a Jewish woman than to fail tradition.

The old maid is seething. Damn Messody and Sol, those two malogradas always hunting for a flaw! What a jealous, sharp-tongued pair they are!

She curses them vigorously: may they turn into billy goats, grow horns, and goatees, and be covered in bile...!

Here comes Mazaltob. Following the custom called *touféra*, she has let her long black tresses down.

That custom, which calls for a woman's mane to be admired before it is forever obliterated under the nuptial kerchief, where does it come from?

God of Abraham, how lovely is the young girl thus!

All of Simi's anger has vanished: She has known Mazaltob since birth and guided her very first steps.

As she comes near the bride, she whispers to her:

"Light of my eyes... my soul... my life... May you be 'sheltered from evil.'[2] May I die in your stead, my dove... And may you be rocking a son within a year."

The guests flock in.

"*Bessinmantob*, David."

"Thank you for your good wishes and may God grant you a long life. Where is your son?"

"He is out of town."

"*No sea su falta*,[3] may it not be his fault, may he never be missed."

Prim and serious as one ought to be for the occasion, Mazaltob and José are in the living room sitting next to each other.

The women will not stop praising Mazaltob's beauty to Mrs. Macías:

"Your daughter is beauteous as the morning sun and her fiancé, too, has quite a noble air to him."

"What a perfect match. May their hearts forever mirror each other, as we say in Tetouan." Uncle Solomon is chatting with Doctor Bralakoff near the couple.

"So, dear doctor, have you had good news from your son?"

"From Serge? Yes, he is soon to be engaged."

"With whom?"

"With a girl from Alsace."

"Is she goy?"

"Not at all. She is Jewish."

"Good . . . ! Congratulations. And what of Jean?"

"He is traveling the world. He recently wrote me from Baku. The boy worries me. He is too idealistic . . . too much of a dreamer."

"Why not persuade him to convert to Judaism? That should cure him."

"Salomon, I've already told you that it is he who is to choose his own religion."

"I was joking. I wish him good health above all."

"Precisely his health worries me. The dear boy has a rather delicate heart."

* * *

Doctor Bralakoff is chatting out loud near the couple with Salomon.

"Mazaltob should have put on more make-up," says a young girl. "She is even paler than usual."

* * *

Time has gone by fast.

Saftaray Saturday is already gone.

On that day, José was required to accompany his future father-in-law to synagogue and pray aloud with him.

From the upstairs galleries, the women threw *dragées* down on the tiles, and the wedding guests congratulated the groom who left shortly after for the Macías home escorted by his friends to savor an adafina, the traditional Shabbat dish.

Mazaltob

In the evening, once tea was served to the rabbis and several other visitors, the women proceeded to sing the customary songs:

> *"This new trousseau*
> *Before thou I shall display.*
> *Mother and sister-in-law*
> *Thou will have nothing to say.*
> *This our bride*
> *Kept a vigil doing embroidery by candlelight."*

The next day was Sunday, the day when the Ketubah is to be signed. The Rabbi read the marriage contract before the two families.

The reading was endless! Tetouan does not marry its offspring lightly.

"Be my spouse, according to the law of Moses and to the law of Israel and with God's help, I will support you, provide you with clothing, give you shelter. For Jewish husbands are required to faithfully support, dress, and give shelter to their wives."

"...And this shall be according to the customs, conditions, and regulations of the Holy communities expelled from Castilla."[4]

It's over: Youssef—known as José—and two witnesses have signed the Ketubah. The Grand Rabbi has approved it with his legal seal.

José, whose own religious practice has long dissipated in the air of Buenos Aires, is unnerved by all that fuss. He sighs and tells himself:

"O Mazaltob...! What one must go through to have you...!"

*   *   *

On Monday, the day of the ritual bath, the women removed all traces of hair from Mazaltob's body. She now resembles a Greek vestal virgin.

Then, at the sound of the you-yous and prayers, she immersed herself three times in the ritual pool of Tebila.

Mazaltob is now clean. She is now pure. She is ready for the man.

A marriage can only be celebrated on a Wednesday following the tractate of Ketubot in the Talmud.

There may be Israelites throughout the world who violate that precept, but not in the holy city of Tetouan.

Tonight—a Tuesday—the bride will be taken to her husband's dwelling.

On the path of the wedding procession all the porches have been whitewashed a few days ago. Sumptuously dressed in the local *Berberisca* costume, a solemn crown called *sfifa* around her head, rouge on her cheeks and henna on her nails, she keeps her eyes closed all the way so that her husband is the first man she will see upon arrival.

Family and friends have preceded her.

The piyyut "Yaalat Hen" rises to the now mostly darkened sky. The entire neighborhood is watching at their windows and doorsteps.

You...You...You...You...

The flower of all flowers has left her home.

With the *nahora*, a huge lantern illuminating its path, the procession courses through the tiny streets of the Judería.

You...You...You...You...

The father bestows on the most prominent men the honor of carefully guiding the blind steps of his daughter.

And Mazaltob, with eyes shut, is led to her destiny.

* * *

An old lady who is José's only relative in Tetouan seems to wait in front of the groom's house. When Mazaltob crosses the threshold, the old woman slips something in her mouth and takes a cup to her lips with these words:

"May your life, o my soul, be sweet and clear as water." You...You... You...

Mazaltob has entered her husband's abode.

The *thalamon*, a sort of elevated throne supported by a few steps, awaits her.

Fervid, if unimaginative, hands have adorned the pillars supporting the wedding canopy with golden gauze. Artificial flowers have been pinned on the armchairs.

Mazaltob, beauty queen, ascends the steps to her throne. Her mother sits by her side. You...You...You...You...

Arab musicians hired to cheer the crowd play their *derboukas* and their *guembris*. A ruffle of chairs, feet, and voices. More and more guests arrive.

Preciada keeps watch to ensure that each receives a share of anisette or of lemon syrup, of cakes or of marmalade. No one should be forgotten, lest malicious gossip run amok! There is a saying in Tetouan for that: "Better to fall into a furious torrent than be caught in foul mouths."

The eldest of the Macíases, who looks more rounded, seems quite changed. Does she look prettier in that way?

Looking at her nose, which appears less protuberant between the now-wider cheeks, one says yes. But if we instead focus on the eyes, which, like teeny-weeny nits, appear smaller than ever, one says no.

But oh how little does Preciada care about her appearance!

So many prayers at the grave of the venerable Rav were at last auspicious: Preciada is no longer the pariah that everyone among her peers feigns to pity.

Preciada is pregnant.

* * *

Tonight the bride will sleep under her new marital roof, following custom. Absent her mother-in-law, an elderly lady of standing remains by her side.

But tomorrow night—for no one would risk upsetting the sequence of the wedding celebrations—Mazaltob will become a woman.

* * *

Wednesday is the day of the *Sibaa berahot*, or of the seven blessings.

At about nine in the morning, José, his father-in-law, and their guests exit the synagogue.

Our forty-something groom wears the required white silk talith over his morning suit, a masterpiece made by an Argentinian tailor. The holy little boxes of his tefillin stand secured by straps to his forehead and his left arm.

Ah! What would his American friends say if they saw him bedecked like this!

As for Mazaltob, she had a near escape, too: these backward Moroccans tried to put her in a Berberisca gown for her marriage...!

But this time, José would not let them get away with it: he had to speak up.

Mazaltob in a gown of black velvet embroidered with gold thread? Absolutely not...! Civilized people wear white. White is virginal—and sexually arousing.

The Macíases had to give in. Surely people will gossip. Nevertheless, several wealthy Tetouani families now follow that European custom...

As he enters his residence, José stands agape and dazzled: Mazaltob, veiled and surrounded by orange blossoms, is miraculously beautiful.

Thinking of the night ahead, the old playboy of Buenos Aires quivers with blissful anticipation.

* * *

The rabbi has now arrived. A silver cup, wine to the rim, is handed to him. The ceremony begins.

At once soft and guttural, Hebrew words shoot out of his long white beard. While the men stand and listen, the bride, head covered, lowers her eyes, those humble eyes unworthy of looking at a rabbi's face, for she is a woman.

As if to better serve God, the rabbi, agitated as a human flask filled with prayers, swings to and fro, chanting, Adonaï's name always on the tip of his tongue.

Wine spills from the overflowing cup. A good omen! The seven blessings will be all the more effective.

The Ketubah is now being read in front of the assembly which acts as witness.

You...You...You...

At last José takes the wedding ring out of his pocket. As in a pass-the-parcel game, the small object moves from hand to hand. Is it made of gold, as required by the Law of Israel?

"Yes," reply two witnesses.

The rabbi takes the band and places it on the bride's right index finger. From that moment on, Mazaltob belongs to her husband.

* * *

The blessing ends with the noise of broken glass. And although everyone knows what it is, questions fly.

"What happened?"

"Nothing. A broken glass."

Shouldn't we be reminded there is no such thing as perfect happiness in the world? We broke a glass so that everyone will think:

34

Mazaltob

"Let us not rejoice in excess. What we possess in this world, God can shatter like glass."

* * *

The whole day will be devoted to the wedding guests. But after a bleak and chilly dinner served in the rabbis' honor, José will be alone with Mazaltob. That same Mazaltob he has kissed only before a witness. Mazaltob, so young...so young...

Mazaltob, bequeathed to him, he already fading in age, by the laws of a country he forgot and even renounced.

Life is beautiful.

Chapter 5

"It is truly extraordinary, Assiba. Her ring is the only piece of jewelry on her."

"Yes, Fortuna, that is extraordinary... And yet this José Jalfon is very rich."

"Assiba and you, Fortuna, are clueless. Mazaltob's ring alone costs much more than what the three of us together are wearing."

"Oh, Bonina, please, what an exaggeration!"

"Not at all, Assiba. May I be struck by lightning and die right now if so...!"

"Oh, Bonina, I believe you. I have already noticed this José Jalfon has got European tastes. But even so, I still think that a woman's neck, ears, and arms should never go unadorned."

"You are quite right, *mi bueno*: one ring, however big, isn't that rather shabby? It doesn't 'show,' as we say here."

In one corner of the room, newly-weds Assiba, Fortuna, and Bonina go on whispering. Occasionally one of them looks away to gaze at Mazaltob, who is lying down on the marriage bed.

"Fortuna, have you noticed how sad she looks?"

"Indeed, she seems not like a bride, but like a widow."

"Perhaps she would have preferred another man instead."

"Another man? You, my dear, are delirious! Who wouldn't want such a well-born husband... And what's more, a millionaire...!"

"Oh, I do not speak lightly: last Tuesday, she did not keep her eyes shut all the way to her husband's house. Her eyelashes fluttered... I am sure of it."

"Is that true, Bonina? Are you sure of that? I would never have thought Mazaltob capable of that."

"Mazaltob, sweetie, is nothing like the girls from here. To be penniless and nevertheless still be chosen by José Jalfon, that's called luck!"

"Oh well, my husband, as you know, is not rich... but I am not envious."

"For God's sake, that's because you simply go by our saying: better ride a placid donkey than be thrown off a horse."

"Thank you for likening Baruch to a donkey."

"Darling, do not be angry with me: you know I love you. May misfortune always befall me, not you."

* * *

Mazaltob, on the large marriage bed nearby, all arrayed in silk and lace, accepts her friends' good wishes.

Her eyes in her very grave face seem to gaze at a place so far away not even a single one of her most inquisitive friends dare to speak of the night before.

In a few moments, the women will respectfully leave the living room to allow for three rabbis, José, and six men of the Macías family to enter and begin the customary prayers. This will be repeated every day until the following Wednesday.

During the eight days known as the *huppah*, Mazaltob must remain in bed, José at home. But at night, under the watch of Mrs. Macías, they must sleep apart.

Where does this custom come from? Compassion for the young flesh?

Surely not, for Mosaïc law imprisons the weaker sex in an infinite nil.

* * *

Is it rather for fear of forever damaging a woman's body, that fragile instrument of procreation?

* * *

"Listen, mother. I have accepted it all until now. But I've had enough. Mazaltob is my wife and I demand that you leave us alone tonight."

Mrs. Macías, turning very pale, looks at her son-in-law. How could he ask such a thing...? He must be joking...

But he isn't. His voice now sour and throaty, he insists:

"Mother, do you understand? I ask that you leave us alone."

Mrs. Macías then begins to shake: her son-in-law is surely mad. Never since Jews were driven out of Spain has there been a husband with a similar request in Tetouan.

But such infamy will only occur over her dead body.

"How dare you ask for that? Especially you, a great grandson of the revered Rabbi Jalfon...? Are you not fearful of God's wrath?"

"Oh," sniggers José, "if God's wrath extended to all Jews who neglect the huppah... In Argentina, the goyim are not the only ones to honeymoon after the wedding. Do you truly believe there is nothing but your mummified Tetouan on earth?"

But Mrs. Macías cares little about the customs of other countries. Tetouan—the city where she and her entire family were born; Tetouan—the city she never left...; Tetouan is the center of the universe for her.

Like most Jewish women, she has never sought to understand the meaning of those religious obligations. She knows only one thing: one must keep doing as is done from father to son. She is trying to have that stubborn son-in-law of hers understand that.

But he suddenly loses his composure, growing ever more impatient with the endless discussion.

"Enough!" He shouts. "You must leave, you understand! I am telling you to leave!" But this time Mrs. Macías is unable to reply.

Her eyes, on her face that's now awfully pale, are closing. Taking her hands to her chest, she then collapses, moaning.

"Oh no, is she dead?" José wonders, frightened.

He is startled: He did not hear her come in, but Mazaltob, very white in her white nightgown, is here.

"Fetch my father," she commands.

*　*　*

When David, her father, comes in, Mazaltob is spraying her mother's face with water. The poor man, seeing his wife's body so still, thinks she is dead.

"Wo...Wo...Wo...*Wo por mi*! Jamila, my soul...! You have abandoned me...! Wo...You have left us, and no one has even recited the *Shemah*—that holy prayer we say for the dying—for you!"

"Listen, father," says Mazaltob, "I think she is still alive."

"Do you really think so? O my dear child, blessed be your voice which gives me back hope..."

"But we must get Doctor Bralakoff at once."

Mazaltob

"You're right, my life. Only you here know to utter sensible words. Go ahead, José, run, run!"

* * *

And José runs in the night.

But one thought torments him. Did Mazaltob hear their discussion, that discussion which caused her mother to faint?

And if she did hear it, will she apprise old David of it...? So many headaches ahead...!

Ah! What got into him when he decided to find a wife in Tetouan!

But could he have imagined that in the twentieth century religion would impose so many ridiculous constraints on a people?

* * *

"There, there, you're now feeling better, aren't you, Madame? But how did it happen?"

"I do not know, Doctor. All of a sudden I felt ill."

"Yes, your heart hasn't been very strong since the birth of your last child. You ought to stop at that, lest you depart for the other world when bringing another child to this one."

"Doctor, I shall do as God wills."

"I knew you would say that. Good old Tetouan ladies! You're all the same...! You must keep watch, David...

"I'll let you rest now and will return tomorrow."

Closing the door, the doctor joins Mazaltob and José, who have been waiting on the patio.

He no longer has that cheerful face he puts on for the ill. It is now dark as the day of Tisha B'Av, which commemorates every year the misfortunes of Jerusalem.

"Mazaltob, my child, your mother's heart is weaker than I had thought... Did she experience today a strong sorrow or an emotion?"

Not looking at her husband, Mazaltob then answers in a broken voice:

"No, Doctor, no. My mother was the same as always today."

* * *

And the days go by.

Nobody suspects that Mazaltob has deserted the large marriage bed. Nobody suspects that José has left the house. Nothing appears to have disrupted the customary huppah.

We know only that Mazaltob's mother is unwell. She has overworked herself so severely for her daughter's wedding!

But Uncle Salomon, Mrs. Macías's brother, is aware of what has happened.

He lectures José:

"Listen, I understand that all these customs may seem childish or foolish to you, for I, too, have traveled. I assure you that I do not approve of the observance of such countless rules, which fashion our God into a rather fastidious and punishing bogeyman. The God we here pray to is alas much more concerned with petty business than with our spiritual selves. Too often He will tell us: 'Purify your body,' but 'Purify your soul,' not frequently enough. Nevertheless, we must not forget, José, that our religion was born in a time when men knew nothing of hygiene.

"Our Legislator, sound as He was, wished to improve the conditions of our terrestrial lives and lengthen them for as long as possible—while awaiting that other less complicated one. Perhaps this sound Legislator could have given us a hint. But none of our simple-minded ancestors would have abided or understood.

"Hence He commanded and He threatened.

"On account of hygiene, He prescribed the circumcision of all sons of Abraham. On account of hygiene, He forbade us certain foods such as pork, game, or shellfish. On account of hygiene, He enjoined us to wash our hands before each meal. On account of hygiene, He said that a bath is as good as a prayer. On account of hygiene, He wished that following the consummation of a marriage, newlyweds be separated for eight days.

"Under such circumstances, you'll likely say that anyone well versed in medicine, regardless of his religion, is as good as the most practicing of Jews. But medicine, which is man's invention, does not have the weight or the persuasive force of the divine word.

"And do not forget that the keepers of traditions, those I like to call the 'custodians' of a religion, are chiefly the elderly, most of whom have never gone past the city's gates . . . !

"Once they arrived in Tetouan after their expulsion from Spain, the children of Israel, in observing the minutiae of the Law, strove to consolidate their bonds, as is often done in a hostile country.

"We could have aspired to a shared ideal. But for many of us, the notion of Ideal is something too abstract. It varies with each individual—that Ideal. And God is like a book: each one of us apprehends Him with his own personality.

"But you see, all nuances disappear when the choice is either to do something or to not do it. Jews, a homeless people against their own will, acquire a sort of nationality by dint of their interpretation, narrow to be sure, not of the spirit, but the letter of the Law. That narrow interpretation is what unites them and counteracts across the ocean the liberalism of our Tetouani motto: 'Wherever you might be, do as you see.'"

"I will not be persuaded, Salomon," replied José. "There are countless free-thinking Jews. Only one thing I know for sure: All of this is meritless in our times."

"Bah! Why such rush?" replies Mazaltob's uncle, great reasoner in front of the Eternal. "Once the older generation is gone, men like you, José, need not be tolerant any longer: our youngsters travel and read a lot."

"But what will happen to the women . . . ? Some, like mine, are already serious readers . . ."

"Women, my dear José, will as always evolve slower. Their actions are pre-conditioned, and self-examination is painful to them. Yes, women—even one like yours—will have a delay of one or two generations from the men. Unless we speed their emancipation by transplanting them to a different place.

"You will figure this out upon your return to Argentina with Mazaltob.

"Isn't that what you intend to do?"

José stands up, however, not giving an answer: his father-in-law has called him for Arbit, the evening prayer.

*   *   *

The huppah ends tomorrow. Even so, José looks somber.

Obliged to contain his desire and his revolt, he now cannot forswear his silent anger.

Not a single word of reproof from his mother-in-law. Not a single word of reproof either from Mazaltob…To the point that he wonders if he hasn't dreamt the distress he has caused the two women.

But their silence eats away at him. And a perpetual uneasiness grips him.

It all starts with the small unease caused by those unusual gestures, by those new cadences to which he cannot grow accustomed. Small unease upon encountering so many men in skullcaps and *lévite* frock coats.[1] Small unease at the sight of women in stiff, inelegant clothing. Unease, too, for his eyes—the eyes of a city dweller—which search around in vain for the smooth lines of a statue, for the loveliness of a vase of gracious proportions, for the brilliant painting that will rouse an emotion.

And a growing unease with a religion which follows every step, intrudes in your life, and controls every gesture. Unease, too, for his different way of thinking. Unease, above all, to know that blame, rebuff, or rebellion, all are useless. Hence to be swept away and slowly crushed by the formidable wheel of prejudice and belief.

And for the old playboy of Buenos Aires, an even greater unease to have a wife who is too pure, a wife to whom vice cannot even be explained, and for whom not a few rituals of a carnal past must be forsaken.

And lastly, one thing to make him deeply uneasy: to know nothing, to understand nothing of this woman whose lips are sealed…And to sense that of her, only her body will he possess…

* * *

Today is the eight-day anniversary after the wedding. It is called "the Wednesday of the Fish," and it marks the end of the celebrations.

Since the huppah has ended, José is allowed to go out for some fresh air.

But the austere Tetouani tradition does not afford him a reprieve on his first outing. This morning, flanked by his perennial, if circumstantial friends, he must go to the market to buy a fish, which symbolizes fecundity.

At home, the fish is placed by nimble fingers on the most exquisite serving platter. It is adorned with paper flowers and lays on the table in front of the wedding throne.

Next, amidst the crowd's cheers, Mazaltob rises from the prison-bed where she has been lying for the last eight days. Once in the living room, she proceeds to remove a few scales from the fish with a knife that has been handed to her.

You...You...You...You...

During the meal, the couple, the family, and their friends will savor with the best sauce that maritime token of fertility.

The wedding celebrations have ended.

In the afternoon, Mazaltob will purify herself in the ritual bath known as Tebila. And as eight days earlier, the man will be permitted to enter.

Chapter 6

Rio Martine in July.

Like a patch of still-golden sky, the porthole-shaped moon seems to peek through its window to gaze at the night.

Billows of seafoam tickle the sand on the beach, while small waves on the horizon waltz with the stars.

Here, the city's narrowing skyline has regained all its dignity, and the ocean's immensity answers to the vastness of the plain.

Far from her family's tents, Mazaltob, sitting on a rock, breathes in the evening air. Two weeks of happiness unfurl before her thoughts like a smooth ribbon, day after day.

* * *

Blessed be this excessive summer heat! Yes, blessed be that heat which has forced the Macíases to escape the stifling city!

* * *

Mazaltob breathes in the evening air.

The soft breeze makes the sea quiver voluptuously in the moonlight.

Did the day leave behind its manifold lanterns to the sky upon the coming of twilight...? Mazaltob is dreaming. The soothing sway of the waves lulls her heartbeat.

Accustomed as she was to the Judería's strict confines, here she finds the sky's boundlessness oppressive. Or perhaps she finds it oppressive because she has never known such bliss. Or just perhaps, at sixteen, she quietly yearns for something that she can only dream of—and that yearning now makes her grow faint.

* * *

Mazaltob

How much preparation, how many worries before they could leave the Judería!

A dozen donkeys were needed to cross the seven kilometers that separate Tetouan from Rio Martine!

Why a dozen donkeys? Some are for the family, others for food, and still others for pots and pans, clothing, mattresses, or blankets.

When the caravan reached its destination, there were about ten tents already on the beach. One could catch a glimpse of a few faces. Everyone, thank God, came from a good family. Luckily, we'll be able to socialize with them—for what would a Tetouani do with his solitude!

And now that we have all but settled and have had our supper, we must, as the last arrived, pay a visit to the families already here.

Several women on the side surround Mazaltob's mother.

Poor Mrs. Macías! . . . Each day her heart is growing weaker, her bones more achy. . . Will she have the strength to deliver her tenth child?

A tenth child isn't all that rare in Tetouan but it is rumored that Doctor Bralakoff gave her tips to avoid a new pregnancy.

But doesn't the Law of Israel forbid that type of practice? Here is what the Doctor presumably told old David:

"Why not simply take a mistress? Another pregnancy would kill your wife." But on that matter the Law is even more stringent!

Nonetheless, David is an inveterate optimist: his wife has safely birthed nine children. Why should a tenth one put her in danger?

Deep inside, however, he isn't all that reassured.

And Uncle Salomon, Preciada, and Mazaltob—all of whom had consulted Doctor Bralakoff—are anxious.

That looming birth, which hangs somewhere between fate and foreboding like a sword of Damocles—that small life which may bring death—is expected in six months.

This is why José's face is more somber than ever: How could he, in moments like this, ask Mazaltob to come with him to Argentina?

True, he could claim his rights as master and demand obedience from his wife, but the Macíases, like every family, have an entente, a unity which blocks his latent cruelty. How could he tear at the intricate fabric of their mutual tenderness and not hurt them?

And don't we say in this country: "One heart is the mirror of another"? Since the tragic discussion of that eventful night, he dares not speak up.

But he feels sick with nostalgia, hopelessly unsuited to the country where he was born, and each day more alienated from it. He is weary of the compulsory prayers, tired of his own repressed skepticism, perhaps bored, too, with Mazaltob, that foreign wife who reveals nothing of her thoughts. He is ceaselessly obsessed with one single thought:

"I must leave ... I must leave ..."

* * *

On the fiery side of the sun, a tufted cloud strolls by, bringing a momentary chill to the lovely weather.

It is siesta time.

Mazaltob, who appears to be asleep in one of the tents, is actually reading.

Although her eyes look closed, she is actually reading a letter...or rather re-reading it.

On that day, she had gone with old Simi as usual to borrow some books from Doctor Bralakoff. The dear man has always guided her through the maze-like universe of novels. His library is even larger than that of the Alliance and he receives the latest books as soon as they are published.

Suddenly, a fortuitous waft of air, and here is what happens next: on Doctor Bralakoff's desk, papers start flying; putting everything back in order, Mazaltob sees her name on one.

First, it's just a casual look, followed by the interior struggle between her conscience and her curiosity. Then, recognizing the handwriting, her eyes race through the lines faster and faster...Then, with eyes shut, the young woman reads:

Dear father,
I have heard of Mazaltob's wedding. I have never felt so sad. Poor little friend of my childhood, so sweet, so understanding, and so beautiful...! Poor little friend of my childhood, whose auspicious name belied her destiny...!
Her youth beckoned to the youth of another, her charm invited only love.

46

Mazaltob

My poor, poor Mazaltob, who discovered between the lines of a book a world beyond her native country where women and beauty reign as queens. May God help her to forget a world she merely glimpsed...

My poor, poor Mazaltob, already married and handed over... and to whom...?

My poor, poor Mazaltob, who was born in Tetouan...!

A tear ran down Mazaltob's cheek. Dear friend of her childhood! Dear Jean who, after two years of absence, still hasn't forgotten about her.

Sweet companion of her naïve years, you, face of light! Your heart was so kind!

She saw him frequently the year before he left. He used to bring to their house those beautiful books from France. He would explain them to her and make comments, the two of them engrossed, leaning over a page.

Before he left, Jean would frequently come to visit, as the Macíases didn't seem to mind: for what would the destiny of a Jewish woman share with that of a non-circumcised?

Yes, Jean felt a great deal of affection for Mazaltob, which she undoubtedly returned... Doesn't she still love him as she loves her brothers...? And yet, he is so foreign to them that she can only love him differently.

How sorry he feels for her in that letter...!

Will he soon return? Wouldn't it be sweet to see those blue eyes, to hear once again his voice? How sorry he feels for her in that letter...!

"Indeed," thinks Mazaltob, "had destiny willed it, I could have been born somewhere else... far, very far from Tetouan..."

* * *

Salomon and Doctor Bralakoff come to Rio Martine for the Sabbath.

"This is quite nice, darlings, though I'll admit that I miss hearing our Jewish 'muezzin' calling for prayer: 'Minha time... Minha time!...'"

"Canana's voice is that of a true stentorian. With him around, nobody could forget his religious duties on Fridays."

"Salomon," interrupts David, "what's new in town?"

"Well, many of us are already out buying those tiny jugs that are customary in the nine-day period prior to the Ninth of Av."

47

"Would you bring some for my little ones, dear brother-in-law?"

"Are you sure, David? Those fragile potteries are given to children in the hope that they will break them and cry when that happens, because the greatest grief and sorrow must be expressed on the ninth day[1] prior to Tish'a Be Av… But God, in my opinion, must be smarter than that… How could He mistake the weeping of a child who broke his toy with that of a devout man who bemoans the Temple's destruction?"

"Oh Salomon, you're so modern!"

"Modern…? Simply because I think that the Eternal must prefer quality to quantity?"

"Oh, dear!" interrupts Bralakoff who has just arrived, "don't you say that! Have you not, excepting your nose, a Jewish bone in you?"

"Doctor, what do you mean?"

"I mean that our God prefers precisely quantity to quality. Think of our prayers, for example: We must go to synagogue three times a day to praise the Lord in every possible way all the while screaming like fishwives. Think also of our weddings. We have to pray before, during, and after. Think of our birth ceremonies, our Bar Mitzvahs, or our deaths… Prayers, prayers, and more prayers. Poor God! How dull He must surely find us… If I were God, I would have sent you all to Hell a long time ago."

"You, Bralakoff, are clearly not from here," says David. "People in Tetouan look askance at you if you're not observant."

"Do you mean observant or spiritual? Oh, David, how well you exemplify this city and its gossip!"

"Perhaps you're right, Doctor. But that is what my ancestors did and, not presuming to know better, I shall do the same as they."

"That means," snickers Salomon, "that if your grandfather got drunk each day on a liter of anisette, you would not wish to improve upon his example, and would similarly drain an entire liter yourself…"

"Well, well! Between you, Bralakoff, and you, Salomon, what company I am in! See what traveling does to you?"

"Well, my friend, a change of air should certainly not harm you… Travel broadens the mind, even at your age… You think small because the horizon is so close in Tetouan that you can almost touch it."

"Jews thankfully have here a few virtues to compensate for their shortcomings!"

"True," concedes Bralakoff, "they do, indeed, have many virtues."

"First," continues Salomon, "our families have strong bonds. Nothing is more revealing than our phrase: 'May I die in your stead.' They would literally pass on to save a loved one. A selfish person is unknown in our households and words such as father, mother, child, brother, or sister are nowhere so meaningful as they are here."

"That's number one," interrupts Bralakoff.

"Number two, we are thoroughly wholesome. Oh, I am speaking not of our physical health, which is preserved by the exacting requirements of Kosher food, but of our moral health. Vice here goes up in smoke. I have never, in my many years living in this city, even heard of adultery. And do you know anyone among our people who would impregnate an unmarried girl? This is why there is no need to champion an illegitimate child: Here, there aren't any.

"As for some perversions or sexual inversions, those venomous flowers of the civilized countries, our sound Tetouan population may not be able to even imagine them . . . !

"To describe our women, there is only one word: honesty.

"Many will find these to be undoubtedly poor ideals. The limited prospect of a husband and children is scarcely a novelist's bonanza! Regardless, there is perhaps some good in not being so civilized."

"Sure, but it depends on your point of view," mutters Bralakoff, who is thinking of Mrs. Macías's perilous pregnancy and of Mazaltob's precocious May-December marriage.

"Well, of course," says Salomon. "As in any prescription you give, Doctor, there are several 'contraindications.' That means only that we have the shortcomings of our qualities. Perhaps we will one day be more perfect."

"More perfect! Hmm . . . My turn, Salomon, to say as you all do here: 'When the Messiah comes . . .'—in other words, not before quite a long time."

In seeing from afar Mazaltob's slim silhouette outlined against the deep blue of the sea and the light blue of the sky, the doctor adds:

"There goes one which Tetouan fortunately isn't gripping as tightly."

"True," replies Salomon, "but will it be in her best interest?"

* * *

"So? Anything yet, Mazaltob...?" asks Mrs. Macías.

Were the young woman not from Tetouan, she would perhaps fail to immediately grasp the meaning of that question. But Mazaltob comes from the Judería, so she answers:

"No, mother... I am not yet expecting."

"That's rather unfortunate since you have been married for four months thus far."

"Do not despair, mother. Think of Preciada."

"May God spare you your sister's lengthy wait. I am eager to see you pregnant. Does a married woman have any joy other than motherhood? For us, women from Tetouan, children are our whole life."

Mazaltob is silent. She gazes somberly at her mother's loins full now of a deadly promise. Yes, for a woman from Tetouan, children are her whole life...

But in other countries, the countries of books, sixteen-year-old women are still harvesting the golden fruits of joy. These women—or rather girls—are still allowed to rejoice in their precious youth and to cherish love before they cherish a child.

Thus, Mazaltob sighs.

Her soul often loses itself on forbidden paths far, very far, from Tetouan.

* * *

"Doctor, here is your *Graziella*."

"Did you enjoy this book, my dear?"

"Yes and no. No because one senses that Lamartine, deep inside, is flattered that the young girl has died for him. And to think that all he can do with the naïve love of the sweet Italian girl is write a book...when silence could have been so priceless! But how I love and envy Graziella! She was nearly my age when she died, but how intensely her heart lived during those few years! Furthermore, she was free... Free to roam under the sky and to run, engulfed by the fragrance of orange trees, with not a single soul to tell her: 'You can't do that.'"

Next to her, the doctor, not answering, gazes at Mazaltob, whose beautiful face is exultant. Does he find it amusing that Lamartine is being read in this remote corner of Africa?

No, Doctor Bralakoff is sad, with the sadness one feels for a butterfly with broken wings.

*　*　*

José has already been in Tangier for a few days.

In going to Rio Martine and seeing the shabby mushroom-shaped tents, the women cooking outdoors, the mules pegged to their posts—all of it a haphazard and prosaic ensemble—he couldn't help summoning up Mar del Plata, the elegant Argentinian beach town.

He recalled the women's light dresses and their silk umbrellas; he breathed in the raw scent of kelp mixed in with that of expensive perfumes. He heard Gypsy melodies, both irritating and tender, answering to the undulations of the surf.

… And awakening at dawn the next morning, he left on his horse.

He rode to Tangier—the big city, delighted to get away from Tetouan and all the family duties. There, too, he found narrow streets, rough pavements, and Jewish women with headscarves. He was deafened by the perpetual *balek, Sidi*[2] in Arabic shouted by the Arabs, by the tinkling sound of coins thrown by Tangier's moneychangers into metal bowls.

But he also saw English women with fine skin, Italian women with beautiful profiles, Spanish women with glossy hair, and smart French women wearing the latest fashions—at last!

He found a music hall to spend the evening, a theater, social clubs, and numerous cafés—in sum, a foretaste of civilization which put his mind a bit at rest.

And since nobody knows him in Tangier, he let himself go. Now he can breathe. He is free not to go to synagogue, free to smoke, to savor shrimp—his favorite! Nobody is there to reprimand him. He can smile to the pretty ladies and, should sadness sometimes grip him, it is only for thinking of the Judería to which he must soon return.

But upon receiving a letter from America which was forwarded to him from Tetouan, he immediately left Tangier for Rio Martine.

*　*　*

"Mazaltob, I have received a letter from Buenos Aires. With no one to manage it, my business is imperiled. A millionaire there today could be penniless tomorrow. I must get back. But since your mother's illness prevents you from following me, I will call for you in a year."

"As you wish, José."

"Is that really all she has to say?" thinks the Argentinian, annoyed. "What! I am leaving to the other end of the world, and she has not a word of tenderness, not a word of regret!"

"As you wish, José."

"Is she a woman or a piece of marble?"

For José thinks too highly of himself to ask: "Did I even try to make her love me?"

If Mazaltob, whose father lost all his money, is not honored to be his wife, she should be put to shame. Let that chaste and cold beauty remain here and gorge herself on foolish novels . . . ! And let him, José, embrace the party of cheer, laughter, and revelry . . .

And then he started reading once again his "business" letter:

Are you dead, or worse yet, are you married, my dear José?

In either case, I should feel very sorry for you, however, if it's the latter, it is you I shall extend my sincerest condolences to. But you, at barely forty, are too smart to leave *ad patres*, and too robust to give up our life of pleasure and debauchery. Myopic as I am, I can hardly envision you, even with a double pair of glasses, as a don who bid his carousing farewell to sit quietly next to a serious madame, she (just between us . . .) moneyed and dowdy in equal measure, and pretentious like you have no idea . . .

Phew! What a long sentence! Blame it on the married ladies. I have no affection for them other than when they have the good sense to become my mistresses.

Do you know that all of the pretty ladies in our coterie keep asking for you? They are so eager for your return that three of the super-duper, mega-lovely gals we've newly become acquainted with are dying to meet you.

"When will that famous party animal finally be back?"

The youngest one, I suspect, would be especially to your liking.

Mazaltob

She is just your type. Funny enough to make even the Pope crack a smile. Blue-gray impish eyes, gold-splattered hair, and the chic of a Parisian. And a two-sided coin: angel on heads, devil on tails.

Now that you've exhausted the gamut of feelings inspired by your native country, get down from your lyrical heights and come back, my dear José.

Hurry. Come back. The party that we will throw upon your return will be the most splendid of your entire career.

Your perfect friend to the bitter end,
Pedro

Jose returned to Tangier, where he boarded a ship for Marseille. He would continue from there to Buenos Aires.

* * *

At Rio Martine, Mazaltob looks at the sea, the beautiful sea she must leave for the dreary Judería.

And Mazaltob has a heavy heart.

Chapter 7

High up on a hill, not far from Tetouan, lies a silent city.

On sunny days one's gaze collides with its sublime whiteness, and the light there seems to linger even on cloudy days.

No cypresses stand like flags at half-mast to mourn the end of hope. Instead, only the rock's silent ascent to Heaven.

This is the Jewish cemetery.

No flowers, no crowns, no monuments to vanity, instead only the bare nudity of death. Graves, all made of freestone to look the same in the afterlife, hint neither at riches nor indigence.

The Jew knows that death is egalitarian.

The poor resting here are assured of keeping their corner of the earth forever, for Israel rejects those dreadful mass graves. Does not a rich man have to pay twice his share to ensure the last sojourn of one who is destitute?

No alleys or paths either. To follow the graves' rigid ascent, the living must toil, puff, and pant. Sometimes, right at the place where the head of the dead is lying to face Jerusalem—the Holy Land—the Five Books of the Law are carved into the stone. An illustrious Rabbi must rest there. High up on a hill, not far from Tetouan, lies a silent city.

* * *

On Friday, a visitation day per Jewish tradition, two women are climbing the necropolis hill in the afternoon.

One of them, slender, elegant, and with limber gestures, assists the other, who bears her enormous belly: the women are Mazaltob and Preciada.

Mrs. Macías passed away eighteen months ago after giving birth to a healthy girl.

Mazaltob

* * *

The epitaphs on the graves, both in Spanish and Hebrew, all look the same: name, date of death, and a few words of praise on the deceased's life. As elsewhere, in Tetouan, one need only die to be regarded as virtuous.

Nevertheless, Mazaltob's mother, like countless women of other races, deserves the following inscription on her grave:

> She spent her entire childhood working, helping her mother to raise her numerous family. Married off at a young age, she kept working, although she did it for herself. Between her fifteenth and her thirty-eighth year, she kneaded more than ten thousand kilos of bread. She prepared more than eight thousand lunches and dinners, spent seventeen thousand hours making preserves, and preparing traditional *alkhalé* or fried meat kept in oil. She formed pasta in the shape of worms to obtain *gousanitos*, cooked grapes for a juice called *aropé*, and distilled figs to make liqueur.
>
> Additionally, she devoted more than seventeen thousand hours to cleaning the house and another seventeen to sewing linens and clothing for her family. She allocated yet another seventeen to soap and to bathe the numerous offspring that she had afforded Israel in the meantime.
>
> She mended more than three thousand pairs of socks. Up early, late to bed, she knew nothing of distractions, not even the most elementary walk. And throughout all those years when she ceaselessly toiled and toiled, she sacrificed her youth and her beauty to that Minotaur called Home.
>
> May she now rest in peace.

* * *

What sadness for the family!

Not only has the Lord deprived Mazaltob's mother in her old age of well-deserved comforts, but he has also, in utter disregard for all of her virtues, inflicted on the devout woman the bitterness of passing on a Saturday.

How sad it is to know that this poor soul will "wander" until the following Friday, the only day of the week when the Gates of Heaven open!

Yomtob Chocron, on the other hand, died merely of old age and just in time for the great happiness of the heavenly kingdom!

* * *

Mazaltob and Preciada have stopped near the grave of Mrs. Macías.

Preciada, weary of hoisting her burdensome load, would like a moment to breathe...

But alas, there are other people there... Especially all those mourners who fill the cemetery with screams and sobs. For in Israel, it is meaningless to say that "profound grief is silent."

The Hebrews, like most Oriental nations, make no secret of their feelings. Grief is measured in a voice's pitch. The greater the sorrow, the higher that pitch.

Hence Preciada, ever fearful of other people's comments, starts moaning out loud, rhythmically syncing her laments with the swaying of her misshapen body:

"Wo...Wo...Wo...Beloved mother! Wo...My eyes...Wo...my light ...What sin did we commit for you to leave us? Was anything denied to you? Did we not feed you chicken broth while you were ill? Oh, mother, you took our soul with you when you departed!"

Preciada has a sharp voice that drills like an auger into your ears.

Impressed and enthralled, the *abelim*[1] assembled in nearby graves direct their admiring gazes towards the eldest Macías.

"Look at her. She is such a good girl!...How dearly she must have loved her mother!"

Preciada indeed cherished her mother and, realizing in moments of solitude that she will no longer see her, she feels as though she is getting punched in the heart.

But for now, she is mostly worried about the scrupulous fulfillment of her mourning duties. Erect, very pale, and her eyes half-shut, Mazaltob doesn't move.

Thus, the women sneer:

"Truth be told, she and her sister are hardly cut from the same cloth; this one will grow a heart only when frogs grow hair."

* * *

No doubt it is because Jews love life too much that their mourning is so rigorous. For someone to whom this terrible event has occurred—to lose life—the living can never know sufficient mortification and abstinence.

"Shiva."

Shiva, the first eight days of mourning...

Shiva, which clothes families in black. Shiva, which requires men to grow a beard and leave their hair unshorn. O Shiva, to satisfy you, the deceased's relatives must sit on icy floors even on wintry days, and on those floors, they must eat their frugal meals. Shiva, O Shiva, your desolation is so profound that you put tears in the eyes of the hired mourners, causing them to lacerate with their nails their feverish cheeks until bleeding follows; Shiva, also named Abel, O Shiva, have you, to honor death, forever killed the smile on Mazaltob's lips?

* * *

The ten months of the year of mourning and their countless rites of bereavement came to an end—but how much grief is enough?

In memory of Mrs. Macías, men recited the Kaddish,[2] for however great the sorrow voiced by women, their prayers are worthless in Adonaï's disdainful eyes.

What's a woman's role? Once she lights a memorial candle to commemorate the deceased's soul in the room where he lies, she must keep watch like a humble vestal to ensure the holy flame remains alive.

She is there to receive callers who come in to present their condolences and who seem intent—especially the women—on making the abelim weep even more.

Unlike Christians, for whom consolation and sweetness are perhaps the most beautiful gifts.

* * *

At the Macíases, Mazaltob has now taken her mother's place.

Nothing is to be expected of Preciada. She gave birth to a stillborn on her first pregnancy—Wo! It was a boy! Her second resulted in a miscarriage...

So, on this, her third pregnancy, Mazaltob's sister dares not even move.

She is afraid of everything: of the brisk air, of the breeze, of the smallest blow, of sitting too hard on low chairs thought to be higher, of slipping on the freshly soaped tiles in the patio.

For peace of mind, she'd keep her belly under a bell jar, if it were at all possible, like a melon. Only one fear keeps her from those other ones: the fear of being the subject of gossip.

That is why, when she is at the cemetery on Fridays to pray for her mother, she'd much rather collapse of exhaustion than be picked apart by foolish talk.

*   *   *

News of Mrs. Macías's death was promptly sent to José in Buenos Aires.

In reply, a few terse lines of condolence arrived from Argentina by mail, followed shortly after by a large bundle of money sent to Mazaltob.

A large bundle of money—as compensation . . . for desertion? For betrayal?

Since then, despite several letters of inquiry, not a word has come from the man who once put a wedding ring on Mazaltob's milky finger.

*   *   *

Nevertheless, there is a glimmer in Mazaltob's dreary life. That glimmer is Léa. Léa the Alsatian, the daughter of Doctor Bralakoff, the beloved wife of Serge.

That delightful creature, with her childlike appearance, her round cheeks, and her perfect pink skin!

Her hands and feet are tiny. Everything in her appearance, even her head's size, rather large for her body, is babylike.

And there is Léa's laughter. It is a sort of impending laughter, always poised at the corners of her lips and waiting for the right moment to burst out for any reason. It's a genuine laughter with no sarcasm, no hint of bitterness. Frank, open laughter, the only one befitting her childish face. Léa, as the expression goes, wears her heart on her sleeve. And although she is petite, the kind girl has a large heart and is always willing to share it with unhappy people.

Léa, following the mysterious law of complementarity, which is also applicable to persons of the same gender, immediately took a liking to Mazaltob, with her nocturnal eyes and her sadness.

And the two young women became friends.

* * *

Léa arrived in Tetouan on her husband's arm nearly eight months ago.

On her husband's arm! That's not done here! And when Doctor Bralakoff, eager to retire, was introducing his son who will succeed him to his friends and clients, Mrs. Serge was freely going on her own about town.

"She goes out alone . . . like an Englishwoman," everyone whispers as she strolls by.

Owing to that, many pursed their lips disapprovingly . . . but that didn't last. Léa has such a lovely, direct manner with all! She also has great respect for other peoples' convictions, such that they have nearly forgiven her permissiveness, which is deemed extravagant in contrast to the women's narrow-minded piety. Indeed, her practice of religion doesn't extend beyond the fast of Yom Kippur.

But can we even expect of her—a foreigner, an Ashkenazi—the same thing we expect of a Tetouani? Isn't it unfortunate enough for the poor girl to belong to the plebeian branch of Israel? The Sephardim, from the word Sepharad, which is the Hebrew word for Spain, view themselves as aristocrats compared to their brethren who are scattered all over the world.

When asked about the reasons for this prejudice—prejudices, as surprising as it may seem, often have an explanation—here is what a Sephardi will answer:

"Our ancestors, Jews from Spain who emigrated from Palestine well before the destruction of the Second Temple, never lived through the terrible siege of Jerusalem. They never experienced the painful humiliation of bearing the yoke of their enemy. Their history had been brilliant until their exile from Spain following the decree of March 1492. They took part in royal councils and set up their tents during military campaigns. They even earned titles of nobility, flaunting coats of arms and vassals of their own.

"Like Samuel Lévy, the fourteenth-century adviser to an Andalusian king, they worked for the public good. Others were royal doctors, renowned astronomers, and many others still, philosophers and poets.

"While the Ashkenazim sought refuge in the ghettos of Russia and Hungary, the gold of our ancestors equipped the ships of Christopher Columbus, who perhaps was himself of Sephardi ancestry.

"During our extended time in Spain, Jewish blood, thanks to countless alliances, was injected into Iberian veins, while through our vessels, Latin blood likewise found its way.

"We know nothing of Yiddish, the language spoken by Ashkenazim, and nothing of Arabic either, a language known only to North Africa's indigenous Jews.[3]

"Instead, we, Sephardim, use Spanish or Ladino (from the word *latino*, which means Latin). Ladino, called Haketía in Tetouan in its plebeian form, is found along the Mediterranean Coast from Tangier to Salonica. Ladino is fifteenth-century Spanish. Hence it sounds impure to modern ears. It is the rallying sign of our brethren all over the world. It is the sacred language of our homes, the holy language in which we translate our prayers.

"We, Sephardim, often have Spanish last names such as Perez, Soto, or Toledano. Several historians even believe that Spaniards whose last name ends in *ez* are descendants of Jewish converts to Christianity whose blood mingled, after the Inquisition, with theirs. We, Sephardim, who consider ourselves heirs to King David's lineage, gave the world Heinrich Heine, Disraeli, and Spinoza, among other names of lesser fame."

And here is what an Ashkenazi may reply:

"We have suffered more than you have. We have been attacked by hordes of Hungarian soldiers and experienced Russian pogroms. We, too, have our great poets and musicians, despite captivity and suffering, which is one of the most ennobling experiences of all.

"If our Yiddish and your Arabic are not as delicate as your Spanish, if our Hebrew sounds more guttural than yours, and finally, if the places we were born are far from holy Palestine, blame only our sad destiny."

But the Ashkenazi will keep quiet because he knows that the slight disdain we feel for him comes not from the heart but from a nebulous tradition. He knows that before Israel's legendary solidarity, "Jew" is a word that bears no epithet.

Mazaltob

* * *

Séty, who is the third Macías girls and is ten, is rocking the newborn baby girl who cries endlessly.

Mazaltob then takes the baby in her arms and starts singing to put her to sleep. What does our lovely young woman sing?

She sings those same songs from Castille sung by her foremothers because Jewish folklore from Tetouan comes chiefly from Romance languages.

Mazaltob sings the romance of Don Hueso, who ambled through Sevilla with a gold bar in his hand. She sings the song of the city of Toledo, where a frail creature once was born, "skinny and of evil intentions." She sings of La Doncella Guerrera, the warrior maiden who won a battle clad in men's clothing and received in marriage the son of King Leon in reward. She sings the tale of Count Velez, who after losing a romantic wager had his heart pulled out for it. And then she sings of the Queen of Moors who wished for a Christian slave, and when she got one, found a sister in her.

And finally comes this other song, *Escuchis, señor Soldado,* a lovely complaint about a woman's faithfulness:

> *"Seven years I have waited,*
> *And seven more years I shall wait.*
> *Fourteen years have passed, and if he still has not returned,*
> *A nun I shall become.*
> *A nun like Saint Clara,*
> *A nun like Doña Inès."*

"Oh, Mazaltob!" says Léa, who has just entered the room, "The sound of your voice is so moving! Where does your perfect grasp of the art of singing come from?"

"I once took lessons with Madame Gérard, the wife of the former French consul."

"Why did you keep this from me?"

"There has been so much sadness in my life. I haven't felt like singing in a long time . . ."

61

Is the young woman alluding to her marriage, or to her mother's death? Léa hopes she will one day find out.

And while Mazaltob carefully puts the baby, finally asleep, in her wicker cradle, Léa continues: "Do you know that I have brought back an excellent piano from Tangier? You, Mazaltob, will sing while I accompany you on the piano. What wonderful moments are in store for us, for Serge, and for my father-in-law, who has missed music for so long!"

"Truth is I seldom spare time for distractions."

"Nay, nay, and thrice nay… I shall help you with your chores… But you, my beauty, you will sing, understand, you will sing!"

Serge's wife gently threatens Mazaltob with her finger, while the latter sadly shakes her head from right to left.

But Léa, not in the least discouraged, insists again:

"You will sing, you will sing, I say! Jean, your childhood friend, and my brother-in-law, who will be here in a few weeks, has seemingly become a talented cellist. He will be surprised and delighted to find such an artistic atmosphere in our dreary Tetouan."

Mazaltob doesn't reply, but her beautiful face is finally relaxing.

And Léa's laughter sounds victorious under the patio's Moorish arches.

Chapter 8

"Samuelito, how much did you pay for these beautiful apples?"

"Two *gordas*,[1] Séty."

"Two *gordas*? . . . Clara, the Carcienteses' maid, paid two *chicas* for them. The truth is that you're not all that clever for a boy."

"You and your foolish girl talk. I am not clever? Me? Ask old Youda!"

"What did you do to that poor man?"

"I only played a trick on him. No harm, no foul . . ."

"What trick? Come on, tell me."

"There, there . . . But first, do you know what we do in Tetouan to keep from falling asleep while watching over a sick person?"

"I have no idea."

"For God's sake, you girls are so clueless!"

"For one thing, I am only ten and you are fourteen. But tell me!"

"Here is what to do to stay awake while watching over a sick person: Place a metal basin on the floor next to the chair where you're sitting. Take a small rock in your hand and hold it tight. Once you're sitting by the sick person's side, let the arm that's holding the rock hang over the basin. If you fall asleep, the rock falls into the basin, making a big 'flop' that awakens you. Everyone in Tetouan uses this method."

"That's very ingenious. But it says nothing of that famous trick of yours."

"Well, here it goes. Old Youda, who used to travel a lot, boasted several times in front of me of having never drunk a drop of non-Kosher wine, forbidden by Jewish Law.

"The old man, who loves to set himself as an example to young people, fearlessly built his reputation on a few lies. When you listen to him, he calls himself a saint and everyone else is the devil. So, having learned that he would keep vigil over one of his brothers who had taken to bed with a fever, I managed to replace the wake-up basin with another filled with non-Kosher wine."

"Oh, didn't he notice?"

"No. The sick person was a bit delirious, and old Youda is very hard of hearing."

"What happened next?"

"So, after the rock fell from the old man's hand, the wine splashed on his clothes, on his face, and even inside his mouth which gapes constantly. And while he was swearing, calling upon Abraham, Isaac, and Jacob to witness his woes, I ran away shouting at the top of my lungs: *Terefa* wine! *Nessekh* wine!"[2]

Little Séty bursts out laughing.

In the meantime, Samuelito turns his face, which now looks worried toward the window overlooking the patio: He has just seen Mazaltob's shadow.

"She is here, Séty," he whispers. "She heard me. I will surely be punished for disrespecting an elderly man."

* * *

But Mazaltob is farther away than we think. Mazaltob is looking in the mirror.

Mazaltob is carefully looking at herself in the mirror.

She first looks at her eyes, her beautiful, slanted eyes, like those of an Asian princess, huge eyes with dark lashes as if lined by thick foliage, deep, splendid eyes, so bewilderingly soft and dark at once.

She then looks at her nose, which is as straight and perfect as that of a statue; she looks at her mouth, which is so narrow it's as if it belonged to a different face. She then examines up close the tight skin on her cheeks in which not a pore is visible, the soft curve of her chin, and the unusually small size of her ears . . .

But Mazaltob doesn't like herself because the small innocent face of her childhood suddenly appears in the mirror lavishly set against a mass of dark hair, like a white camellia inside the folds of a dark velour.

What a beautiful glossy mane, with tresses that so delicately graze her shoulders!

* * *

Mazaltob

Mazaltob looks at her image, thinking she is "a woman from Tetouan."

The scarf covering half of her forehead undoes the beauty of her face, truncating its harmonious proportions and giving it a hard edge. Her ears, peeking out on either side of the fabric, lose some of their grace.

What a dismal kerchief, also known here as *pañuelo*!

What a dismal kerchief designed so that a woman's face, lacking the ornament that hair, whether wavy or straight, usually provides, will be less beautiful!

How many men have wandered through a cascade of blonde locks or in a maze of long dark tresses and lost themselves! How many kiss curls have lived up to their name!

"Women, you mustn't be too pretty," say Israel's sages. "Since we cannot hide those eyes often bewitching to men, we shall cover your hair to diminish your seductive powers. That will result in fewer temptations, and you will steer clear of adultery, that terrible sin."

That is why in this year 1908, most "kosher" women cover their hair. Some women are even twice as kosher: they wear a wig made of black silk known as *crinches* under their headscarf so as to conceal the hair root above the ears, which often peeks through the fabric.

Other more modern Tetouani women find a way around the problem by ordering full-head hairpieces from Paris. That certainly does the trick. These ladies uphold the Law while also retaining all their charms.

*   *   *

But Mazaltob has no time to order a hairpiece, because Jean will arrive tomorrow. Purposefully untying her kerchief, which she then tosses away, she grabs a comb and styles her hair in the French fashion known as *bandeaux*, parting it in the middle and looping it back at the sides, a low chignon at the nape.

Her face is like a beautiful landscape suddenly brightened by a blaze of sunlight.

And like Faust's Marguerite, Mazaltob laughs on seeing how lovely she looks in the mirror.

*   *   *

65

He has seen sun-drenched Africa and the sacred rivers of dreamy Asia. He has seen the milky infinity of wintry Russian plains, experienced sheer rapture in Italian fairylike gardens, heard the majestic rumbling of Swiss waterfalls, delighted in verdant England, its emerald green akin to that of cardboard sheepfolds, and listened to Spain's moving *malagueñas*, which made him by turns laugh and cry.

But above all, he discovered France. He beheld fierce Brittany, which only gives herself to those who love her, greenery-filled Normandy, Île-de-France's shimmering skies, soft-hued Touraine, melancholy Dauphiné, and the Riviera's flashing-blue sea.

His skin drank the wind of open seas and burned at the sun's kisses.

He contemplated for hours a willow's quivering reflection in a pond.

He became intoxicated, to the point of dizziness, with the scent of flowering magnolias.

He visited museums, and joy engulfed him as he stood before their masterpieces. He touched with his eyes the shapeliness of a statue until its softness nearly made him swoon.

He thought that he had captured all the beauty in this world with his eyes... But now he no longer knows...

He no longer knows what he has seen... he no longer knows what he has admired... He doesn't even know what he has loved.

He is looking at Mazaltob's eyes.

And yet...

In all of his travels, how many women's faces have trembled between his hands!

Orbs the color of turquoise or sapphire, amethyst or emerald, golden orbs. Eyes full of languor or full of malice, they were for him no more than pretty eyes. But in the black diamond eyes of his childhood friend, a tender force beguiles him and enchants him.

He recalls having experienced their spell even as a very young child. And now, a mysterious breath overwhelms his manly essence.

Jean beholds Mazaltob.

And in his daze, a single thought comes upon him:

"I can never exist away from Her eyes."

* * *

Mazaltob

No wheels, no horses, no honking. All the same, the Judería's narrow streets are oblivious to silence.

No daydreaming allowed. A window singing: You-You, a door answering: Wo! A synagogue chanting, a passing funeral talking back—Tetouani kindness knows nothing of this dreadful sight: a casket that none should follow.

And there are the noisy Bar Mitzvah processions and the even noisier wedding ones. Behind walls, sharp voices recite something in Hebrew, others in French, while still others chatter in Spanish.

In the night's calm, the slightest noises from outside reverberate inside the houses.

And around five in the morning, the boy who works at the public oven furiously knocks from door to door, asking to collect the bread to be baked.

The Judería? You can't escape it. It seizes you not only by the ears, but by the nose, too: scents of anisette, of melted honey, of clover and cumin, all of which overpower the confined air of its narrow streets—so narrow that there the wings of Poetry cannot spread.

* * *

Nevertheless, in his little room, between a cello and an easel, Jean, his head between his hands, chases a dream.

It's a persistent dream, a dream shattered a hundred times by reality, but a dream, nonetheless. A dream in which, like the beads in a priceless necklace, an endless string of lovely eyes continuously passes by. Beautiful eyes, so bewilderingly soft and dark at once!

And then a voice in that dream says...what exactly does it say? Jean is unsure. But the voice is so deep, so warm, and so tender that the young man's heart shudders.

Are the lamentations he suddenly hears a Dream, or are they Reality? Perhaps they warn of future pain?

* * *

Mazaltob's deep voice now blends inside Jean with distant weeping. And then the dream vanishes...

Jean is in his room once again.

* * *

Outside, howling keeps filling the streets in pressing waves at first, which swell into cries and shouts, and then die off with moans.

Coming closer to the window, Jean sees in the house across the street a woman gloomily rocking her upper body while sitting on the floor.

She personifies grief itself, that Jewish grief which knows no stillness.

"She has been unable to find solace since the death of her husband three years ago," it is rumored in town.

"Three years! And still a sorrow so fresh!" ponders Jean.

But from the depths of his childhood, widows and abandoned women, all of them inconsolable, come to his mind. Each one of their lives is spent, with no hope for renewal.

Many, however, still possess the charming face of youth and beauty. Love itself would revel in their fluttering lashes against its cheeks. These women could no doubt rekindle the flame of happiness and illuminate once again their darkened homes.

But the Jewish woman from Tetouan spiritually withers when desertion or death plucks her husband.

The Jewish woman from Tetouan must not remarry.

The Jewish woman from Tetouan, barring rare cases, has but a single man in her life.

* * *

"You seem so sad, Jean. Are you weary of Tetouan already?"

"Tetouan, Léa, is my place of birth, and the time that weighs the heaviest in our life is, as you must know, when we are lighter in years. That is why I cherish this town, despite all that I find appalling about it.

"Nonetheless, I will confess that I would not like to stay here for long. I am already nostalgic for the scent of grass in the air, for birdsong, and vast horizons."

"Oh, as for me, dear, I am not all that complicated, Viennese bread is the only thing I miss! Such a strange place, this town! We can't even find a bakery here! I had no choice but to knead bread as my neighbors do... But oh, how I prefer bread from the stores of my native Alsace!

And sadly, having a sweet tooth, I get homesick most when I think of our wild strawberries, our blueberries, and our raspberries..."

"Yes, few here have tasted such fruits. But you, Léa, with your fierce independence, must have other more serious opportunities for unhappiness..."

"True, but if most people suffer when transplanted to a new setting, it's because they wish for others to adapt to them, instead of their striving to adapt to others... But I, my dear, doing all things backward, chose to laugh at what should have made me weep.

"Knowing that my voice finds no echo in this atmosphere, which differs so greatly from that of my native land, I could have withdrawn like a snail in its shell, as many others would. However, this form of narcissism not being to my liking, here is what I thought: 'If in any given circumstance, people here act in ways different from yours, must you thus infer that you are superior to them?'

"Pride, my dear Jean: such is the impediment. One need only remove the blindfold with which pride covers our eyes to understand... and perhaps even love..."

"Oh Léa, how I envy your happy disposition! But how could you even speak of understanding when so many things here are baffling?"

"Baffling only because we let them be that way... And because our brain, like an emporium, has on offer ready opinions with which it judges such matters.

"We often fabricate our views and our prejudices en masse... We are like captains who maneuver their boats the same way regardless of the weather. As for all that belongs to the past, it is little different—for when we say: 'this is foolish,' perhaps it is we who are judging foolishly."

"I admire you, dear sister-in-law... In my case, I have an exacerbated sensibility. I suffer first and think after. Pain before reflection: that is, unfortunately, an unchanging principle for me..."

"Oh, Jean! You must be in one of your gloomy days... For the sake of gallantry toward me at least, would you please be more cheerful? I have enough with Mazaltob..."

"Mazaltob... Has she at last heard from her husband?"

"No, he must be a bit mad."

"A bit? Say instead: completely mad...Can one have a Mazaltob in one's life...and leave?"

* * *

That night Preciada "gave light," as the Tetouanis say, which means she gave birth.

This time, everything went well, and the child appears strong. Nevertheless, not a single you-you greeted this new member of the select club of Life.

When people knock on the door to ask about the baby's gender, they receive this sorrowful answer: "Nothing, just a girl."

The same question is asked twenty or thirty times, and each time, it's the same answer: "What did she have?"

"Nothing, a girl."

"Nothing, a girl." All of Israel is contained in these three words. The severity of its Law goes as far as to assign sixty-six days of uncleanliness to the woman, following the birth of *una hembra*. But that period consists of only thirty-seven days if, instead, she has a boy.

A woman? She cannot praise the Almighty or recite prayers for the dying, and neither can she shut the eyes of a loved one.

A woman? To move up the ranks in life she must grow old and resemble not at all the "sickly child twelvefold impure" described by Alfred de Vigny in his poem. Only then, physically transformed, will she be permitted to enter a synagogue or embrace the dead who have been previously cleaned and purified.

"Nothing, a girl."

Preciada, who before her mother-in-law's sour face, dares not smile excessively to her baby, resumes her complaining, as per her habit.

"Wo...Wo...Wo...! The evil eye is again upon me! Won't I ever listen to the you-you's of ritual circumcision when a boy is born? Wo...Wo... Wo...May God spare me!"

"Besides, you could have another girl next time, too," snickers a jowly-faced gossip.

"Be quiet, malograda," replies Preciada. "Don't you dare open Satan's mouth!"

Mazaltob

* * *

Jean is jotting down his travel impressions in a thick notebook.

He might perhaps publish them one day, as his friends think him a talented writer. For the time being, however, he wishes primarily to consign to paper his different feelings in the various environments he has visited. He loves to collect the legends of each country along with folkloric tales so powerful that they express its local scent and color.

But amidst the prose within the cloth-bound notebook, there are oases of poetry where the young man's vibrating soul gushes forth, swells, and then peters out. Jean, a poet in his spare time, knows how to write verse.

Suddenly, the door opens, and Léa appears.

"Ha-ha, mister wannabe author! How are we doing on your travel notes? Have you written anything about Tetouan?"

"Truth be told, sister-in-law, no. I don't find Tetouan very inspiring."

"That's a mere unwillingness on your part. You would have no difficulty gathering loads of fascinating stories here."

"Like what?"

"Let me tell you for instance what I just witnessed: Old Tamar, my neighbor, who has a son in America, has just received a letter from Brazil.

"She can't read, but seeing just then a babouche peddler she hardly knew, she called on him:

'Mi bueno, kindly read me what this says...and may you live to be one hundred.'

The fellow takes out his eyeglasses from his bottomless pocket, sticks them on his large nose and grabs the piece of paper, carefully examining the writing on it. His eyes run from top to bottom of the page and make their way back from the last line to the first, after which they proceed again from right to left, as when one reads Hebrew, and finally from left to right, as one does for books from Europe...

"But how difficult it is for a man—and especially a Jew—to humiliate himself before a woman in confessing he cannot read Latin script!

'So,' presses the old lady, 'come on, speak...Is it bad news?'

'Well, what can I say,' replies the fellow in a loud sigh. 'Amid all this white, dear, I see only black.'

71

'Only black? O God of Abraham, do you wish me in mourning? Wo…
Wo…Wo…my darling son! Wo…Wo…Wo…

Woe is me, his unfortunate mother.'"

That is probably the first time in Tetouan's history that the gloomy
sound of Wo concludes with a chortle.

Jean, overcome by the cheerfulness of the young woman, cannot help
laughing, too. Finally, when the calm returns:

"You're right, my dear. Such a delicious story could happen in no other
climate but Tetouan. It is indeed typical of here, and I shall not forget it."

"Allow me to read the one you were writing when I came in," says Léa,
leaning her inquisitive head on the handwriting of her brother-in-law.

"No, it's not ready. Later…" says Jean.

But the Alsatian girl has a quick eye and, between two pirouettes, she
asks, not in the least offended:

"Funny, Jean, I had no idea that cities or countries could have women's
names…Where is that land called Mazaltob?"

* * *

"My dear Jean, will you forever remain between a rock and a hard place,
so to speak? Do you find it amusing not to choose a religion and not
care what type of characters—Latin or Hebrew—one day will compose
your epitaph? Alas, you are in all likelihood an atheist, like too many of
our youngsters."

"Why so much irony, Salomon, especially given the subject? No, I am
not an atheist. But the God I love is neither Christian nor Jewish.

"The God I love is in my eyes the greatest of all…Precisely because
he is God…and nothing else."

"Too much infinity crushes the human creature, my friend. A God
without a Bible is too remote…"

"You're mistaken, Salomon. He is not too remote because, among all
Gods, my dream reaches out to Him alone."

Chapter 9

Léa is eagerly awaiting Mazaltob, to plan with her a small musical soirée as a surprise for Jean.

But despite her desire to see her friend, Mazaltob, overworked with the approaching Passover holidays, is unable to escape for even one minute the clutches of the home.

What drudgery for women—and especially for Jewish women from Tetouan—what worries and responsibilities! Who will ever praise them for all of it?

If the Mosaïc religion, born more than five thousand years ago, hasn't vanished from the face of the earth, it likely owes this not to its male but to its female devotees.

A preference shared by every woman for small things over great ones, a credence, born of their very weaknesses, given to superstitions—"Were I to infringe upon the Law of Heaven, the Almighty might snatch away one of my loved ones in punishment"—, and finally, the intellectual idleness of Eve, who forsook her ability to think under Adam's tutelage in every latitude—all have turned Israel's daughters into stern guardians of a religion that either ignores them or despises them.

What does Mazaltob, deep inside her, think of the Laws of Moses? No one knows. But she acts in every circumstance as her mother or her sister would.

Is that hypocrisy?

No. But we do not shirk the habits of our childhood, our social environment, or an imitative devotion inspired less by thought than by reflex.

The Bible (Exodus, 23:15) commands that the holiday of Passover be celebrated for seven days. And now it's nearly two months since she began preparing for those seven days . . .

First, she had to get new clothes for the children. Everything—from underwear to hat and socks—must be new.

We must also whitewash, or *encalar*, exterior façades and interior walls of the house.

It's a period of BIIIIIIG cleaning... Nothing must elude the many-eyed Argus, the lady of the house, who rules over the chaos, brandishing her spiderweb brush like a military banner. Cleanliness from start to finish, but above all a painstaking search for *hametz*, or fermented flour, the removal of which is the very reason for the holiday of Passover.

When Jews, under the hand of God, left the land of Misrayim,[1] there was no time for their bread to rise. So, in their haste, the Jews took the unleavened dough with them.

"Moses told his people: Remember the day you departed from Egypt, the house of slavery, for it is with a powerful hand that the Lord brought you out. You will not eat bread that has leavened." (Exodus, 3:1).[2]

Thus, Passover is a commemorative holiday.

The domestic revolution has broken out at the Macíases. If only Simi the maid could be here!

But the poor woman, due to a strong emotion, has been bedridden for the past eight days.

The most remarkable thing is that all those who know of her adventure can't help laughing and commiserating at once.

Here is what happened:

Old Simi, who cannot afford to live in the Judería, has a small dwelling near the city's gates. One night as she was preparing to go to bed by the faint light of her oil lamp, she heard a noise on the patio.

Through the cracks in the door, her wavering eyesight made out three Arab turbans, which stood above three sinister-looking faces.

Thieves!!!!

And nobody around!

Realizing there would be no help coming from this earth, the wretched woman raised her eyes toward the heavens and called out for the saints:

"Abraham! Isaac! Jacob!" She begged with all her ardor: "Rescue me, hurry!"

The thieves became scared: What! This poor woman whom they thought lived alone actually had three men to protect her?

The place had now become dangerous...

And with no time to take anything with them, the three burglars rushed to the door and vanished in the darkness of the night.

"Only faith—literally—can save us," said Léa when she heard the story.

* * *

Early in the morning and alone, Jean sets out for the countryside.

A warm breeze is blowing from the South and the sun, which shows its face between passing clouds, is like a coquette who, between the flutters of her fan, flashes a smile.

Jean sets out for the countryside early in the morning. Alone. Alone? . . . No, not alone, for the invisible presence of Mazaltob keeps him company.

To see her eyes . . . Those eyes whose somber light cancels out daylight for him!

To see her eyes whose burning seal has branded his soul!

The Judería is nothing but a huge dwelling, and its walls, necessary for the privacy of its inhabitants, are even more translucent than mica.

Mazaltob is young. So is Jean. She is a woman. He is a man. That's enough to start gossip.

When he has reached the bridge over the river Martin, the young man stops to watch the silvery liquid at the mercy of the current's fury.

On the water's edge, young Arab boys bathe, and the water dribbling down their coppery skin gives it a shimmering luster.

Jean gazes at the naked children.

What beauty! There isn't a single place on this earth, however destitute, which does not retain a glimmer of its fleeting splendor.

In the glory of early morning, the small bodies appear so harmonious and limber that Jean, beguiled, reaches into his pocket.

His pencil now races on the coarse-grained paper.

* * *

"That looks lovely, mi bueno."

"You really think so, Eliaou?"

"Yes. And I recall that not long ago, when you used to bring books to my sister Mazaltob, you were already making some charming scribbles . . .

75

Or at least, so I thought. As a good Tetouani, I know nothing of those matters."

"And how is everyone at home?" asks Jean, thinking, rather: "How is Mazaltob?"

"Fine. Despite my father growing old and Mazaltob, weary of her heavy domestic burden, becoming increasingly pale each day. As for me, I am plagued with worries..."

"What's the matter, Eliaou?"

"Here is the problem: I am smitten with a young girl from a family that we call here *basha*,[3] that is humble, and my father is of course opposed to the marriage... But having finally found happiness, I won't let it slip away."

"Are you thinking of being disrespectful to the author of your days? The Judería would never forgive you."

"You, my friend, are so naïve that it is as if you hadn't yet cut your umbilical cord... I have a secret card in my game: it's called the Kiddushin."

"The Kiddushin? Forgive me, Eliaou, but I do not recall exactly what it is."

"It is simply the art of getting married despite resistance, by putting a gold band on the ring of the chosen woman. This must be done before two witnessing accomplices."

"But is a marriage not blessed still valid?"

"Perfectly valid. But I beg you, Jean," says Mazaltob's brother, who all of a sudden regrets saying too much, "promise that you will not betray me."

"Have no fear, Eliaou. I would be sorry to cause you any trouble. I've heard nothing."

Thanks to this secret, a kind of friendship bonds the two young men.

Pen in hand, Léa's brother-in-law turns to his interlocutor, whose face is so typical:

"Would you like me to sketch you?"

"I would love it."

* * *

A few strokes and there is an eye: a large eye, round and protruding, which signals a Jew much more than does a nasal appendage—indeed, countless kings have had aquiline noses. And here is a slightly receding chin and somewhat plump lips. And finally, here are, framing the mouth and lending it a sad expression, those two distinctive creases of the wandering race.

"That's exactly me!" marvels Eliaou. "You'll have to come to the house and sketch all of us."

And Jean, addressing a smile to an ever-present Mazaltob, acquiesces: "I will."

* * *

"If you'd like to document your 'travel impressions,' Jean, come with me to the neighbor's house. She is giving *una bodita*, a small party, in honor of her son's stye."

"In honor of her son's stye? What does that mean, Léa?"

"Ah! Ah! You don't understand? I'll explain it to you.

"Little Aaron has a stye. That ailment, presumably transmitted to him by *los de abasho*,[4] is, as you know, very tenacious. Recovery is often followed by re-infection.

"In order to end it once and for all and to appease evil spirits, tiny cakes are baked to simulate a celebration.

"If the blister is on the upper lid, the lid is said 'to have produced a boy.' If it's on the lower lid, it's believed to be 'a girl.'

"If it's the latter—this being Tetouan—the supply of sweets is notably less plentiful."

"But in the end, what happens to all the sweets?"

"Well, we put some in the basement—which is presumed to be near the dwelling place of 'those from underneath.' On good terms with the invisible spirits, we then go back to the patio, where on the table a light meal is served."

"Under no circumstance would I miss such a ceremony, dear sister-in-law. Tomorrow, I am your man."

* * *

The small celebration is over, and while the children, sated with pastries known as *dulces* or *douceurs*,[5] chase each other in the patio's arcades, Léa's neighbor discusses the events of the week.

She first talks about old David who must remarry.

"He isn't young," says someone.

"True," answers an elderly lady. "But is he old enough to no longer think of women? Chastity isn't for men."

"Oh! Sister Simha, you must have a fiancée in mind."

"And why not? The Azouelos have a daughter..."

* * *

General outcry:

"She limps."

"She is thirty."

"Thirty? In each one of her legs perhaps!"

"She is ugly."

* * *

Old Simha then replies somewhat angrily:

"Don't you think I am aware of all that? Oh, for God's sake, you're quarreling as if old David was a real catch! His riches are long bygone."

"Moreover," adds a woman who wears crinches, "nobody works harder, is more even-tempered, or is more frugal than Sol Nahon."

"Yes," snickers a skeptical fellow. "As our saying puts it: saints are economical—they do not eat, drink, or wear out their shoes."

"Poor Sol! Here is a sun[6] which Mazaltob would no doubt eclipse."

Mazaltob... Her name is on everyone's lips. Nevertheless, her face is sad as the Hevra Kadisha.[7]

"Unlike Sol, who is always happy. You must, by the way, know the saying: A smiling face is half the meal."

"To go back to David's daughter, you must have noticed she isn't wearing her headscarf anymore."

"It was certainly a shame to hide such beautiful hair," says a young man.

"If she thinks her hair so beautiful, why agree to cover it? And why uncover it after two years of marriage?"

"That's unheard of..."

"It isn't auspicious."

"Come on! Her first name, and even her last name—which means Messiah—will protect her."

"Has it been a long time since she took off her headscarf?"

"Not at all... It has only been three weeks."

Mazaltob

Making himself very small in the corner, Jean shudders: only three weeks...

He came to Tetouan exactly three weeks ago...

* * *

Tonight, Chopin's melancholy soul floats over the Judería's prosaic walls.

Léa sits at the piano in the dimmed lamps of the *petit salon*. But is that really Léa, that serious young woman who puts up a mournful face?

Mazaltob is nearby.

For the first time since the beginning of the mourning period, she has pinned a mauve collar to her bodice and that soft grounding makes her profile look more splendid.

In the discarnate whiteness of her face, her eyes erupt like two somber stars. Never has beauty looked so moving.

Jean, dark circles under his lower lids sealing his torment, is also in attendance.

Jean is here, drinking in Mazaltob. But despite the magnetic force of her brown gaze, he once in a while shuts his eyes as if unable to conceal some secret sorrow.

Between two notes, we hear thunder rumbling in the distance.

And sometimes a light shiver passes through the body of the young man.

* * *

A note weeps. A note dies.

The "Nocturne" has just ended.

The pianist rises:

"You look unwell, Jean. Perhaps we should stop the music for the night."

"My dear Léa, no, go on. That melody, on the contrary, soothes my poor nerves, which have been so uneasy today."

But Léa sits back, preludes and signals Mazaltob to approach. Unparalleled and affecting, Mazaltob's contralto voice, its modulations by turns deep or delicate, meanders through the melody like a clear winding river.

There, on his chair, Jean, annihilated, fervent, listens.

First, he feels as though silken kisses alighted on his happy soul.

Then, the kisses grow softer... ever softer, and that softness suddenly becomes torture. Outside, the storm is raging and swift lightning slashes the sky through the window.

Mazaltob is singing.

The storm...the music...her voice...Especially her voice...

The sounds now lengthen out onto sorrowful *tremolos*, unsettling Jean's already frayed nerves. An irresistible and dreadful rapture grips and tightens the throat of the young man.

Once the melody vanishes, Mazaltob and her companion turn toward Jean who, collapsed on the chair, seems dead.

They lay him on the sofa. A shadow emanating from the lamp's chiaroscuro hollows out his eyes. His cheeks are white as a lily's petals.

The two women busy themselves next to him. While one of them moistens his temples with icy water, the other fans him and takes his pulse.

"Ah," bemoans Léa, "what misfortune! Why is it that just on this night Serge and my father-in-law are nowhere to be found? I confess that I am rather uneasy...especially nervous as he is...and with his weak heart..."

Mazaltob sighs. She reminisces about that time when on a similar night, she was moistening the pale forehead of her unconscious mother.

...Her mother, afflicted with the same illness...

But Léa quickly gathers herself:

"Why am I so 'dopey' tonight?" She castigates herself. "Instead of whining, I'd better prepare him a cordial."

"You're right, my dear. Run to the kitchen. I'll keep caring for him meanwhile..."

* * *

Léa has already vanished.

Mazaltob leans over Jean, whose breathing she hardly hears.

Jean, her childhood companion, the only person who touched her soul when she was a child, the one who, through the books they read together, traveled with her to the marvelous land of fairies and of lovers...

Jean! He embodies all that is sweet and lovely in her life!

But how white he looks...God, will he die?

The young woman leans closer, as if pouring out her anguish over his motionless head.

80

Mazaltob

The brown bandeaux of her hair almost graze his blonde curls, and suddenly, from her dark eyes, a tear gushes forth and rolls down the young man's translucent forehead.

And then, all at once, Mazaltob feels that her hand is held captive.

And her eyelids quiver because Jean's lips lay on the naked flesh of her fingers. Endlessly.

Chapter 10

Mazaltob, using Passover preparation as an excuse, hasn't yet returned to Léa's house.

Bah! What does Jean care? Doesn't his sketchbook permit him entries to the Macías's home? But alas, as if by design, he was barely able to glance at Her, the dream weaver of his nights and of his days.

How many things would he like to say to her nonetheless!

Is it work that preoccupies the young woman? Is chance to blame, each time disrupting, as soon as it begins, their touching tête-à-tête?

As days unfurl one by one, Jean thinks Mazaltob is avoiding him. But why should she avoid him?

Is it the modesty of a surprised soul?

Wasn't his kiss respectful, that kiss his manly lips could not hold back?

Oh! That night of music and of storm, which her eyes illuminated even more than lightning . . . Oh! That night of all nights in the world in which he thought he would die as he listened to the Revelation of her Voice!

* * *

And then, all went dark inside of him . . . and, like a woman, he fainted. Oh! His poor heart . . .

His poor heart forever wounded during a night pogrom so long ago.

Oh! That other night of his life, that cursed night when his mother died under a *moujik*'s blade for adoring only one God.

Night of hatred, night of terror, which left an indelible stain on his sick heart and on his frayed nerves.

* * *

For Jean, who is oversensitive—doctors would say he is a great hyperaesthetic—there is a limit, lest he suffer, in how much beauty or

82

ugliness he may withstand. His admirations must be measured, his dislikes mitigated, and his daily life regulated and uneventful.

His soul is a wind harp. He wrote that himself, by the way, in a poem
written in adolescence, which begins as follows:

> *My soul is a harp—oh how doleful it is!*
> *A harp vibrating with every breath of air.*
> *Its joys are too sharp and only last an instant.*
> *My soul is a harp—oh how doleful it is!*

... Doleful in suffering... doleful in joy...

Since that long gone Russian night, Jean carries in him a frail heart,
which the slightest shock could shatter...

* * *

Passover is here, and the Judería is blooming—inside the homes.

Passover is here, with its seven days of rest and of rejoicing, its unleavened bread, those *matzot* made of select wheat, picked well after the
rainfall, and its *haroset*, or small orbs made with fruits and spices.

Tonight, during the meal, the head of the family reads the Haggadah,
a portion of the Bible[1] in which are recounted the sufferings of Israel in
Egypt as well as its escape under Adonaï's guidance.

When reading the episode about the Red Sea, it is customary to
break the flourless bread in two to better commemorate the miraculous
separation of the waters.

At the Kiddush—or blessing of the wine—each one of the guests will
have a glass to drink from instead of a single cup.

And once the prayers are over, we will wish one another:

"Next year in Jerusalem."

* * *

Old David, who lately has been in the flour business, has sold the key to
his store to a non-Jew.[2] It's a provisional sale, and he will be able to buy it
again once the holidays are over. Those with a stock of hametz customarily
engage in that practice to elude sin. Old David is one of them.

Isn't it precisely to elude sin, even in intent, that he became engaged to Sol Azouelos, that old maid?

No wedding must be celebrated during the thirty-three days following Passover, but past that period, the Macías family, who is of "high" birth, will be able to marry into the Azouelos family, of equally "high" birth.

* * *

It is the night of Mimona—Passover's epilogue. The Macías's patio is resplendent with light. At the center of a table adorned with flowers and garnished with sweets sits a brass platter filled with flour, inside of which are buried gold coins. That mound of flour is punctured with wheat sheaves, symbols of abundance for the coming year. Above all, may rain fall! A Tetouani saying puts it best:

"When I have no water, I drink water, but when I have water, I drink wine."

On that night, the Judería, following tradition, brims with activity, each family visiting another as if in a game of musical chairs.

And Léa, escorted by Jean and by Serge, who is eager to "get a sighting," goes to Mazaltob's house.

* * *

Few people are at old David's house. It is still early, and dinner time isn't over at the Judería. But Uncle Salomon is there.

Pointing at the flour bowl, Serge, who is just behind Léa and Jean, exclaims:

"Ah! Ah! We may not be poets, but we are no doubt well versed in symbolism."

Somewhat grumpy, Salomon replies:

"Not poets... Not poets... That remains to be seen!"

"You are not possibly saying that we are sentimental, my friend!"

"Excuse me," says Salomon, "but I most certainly am. It is sentiment which dictates that 'lamb not be cooked in his mother's milk.' And it is sentiment, too, which teaches our rabbis to slaughter poultry so as not to make them suffer."

"What a plea, my dear Salomon!" says Serge, laughing. "You are the Don Quixote of our religion."

"Don Quixote? Indeed. I go to war against the windmills of bias and of prejudice...We need to fight against countless myths—for instance, the one that says we have no courage. And yet we, like others, can die for our ideals. But must you think us cowards, simply because our people are not innate warriors, or because we prefer the sweetness of peace to the horrors of battle, or perhaps because we shy from bloodshed?"

"Cowards? Perhaps... Statistics have indeed proven that our people count the lowest percentage of murderers..."

* * *

Jean, who has drifted far from the discussion, suddenly chimes in:

"Why take things so seriously?" he says. "Must the earth not one day close in on the accusers as much as on those accused?...The graves know it: there is no point in anything."

* * *

Mazaltob has just come in.

Is it because she heard Jean's last words that Mazaltob's eyelids imperceptibly flutter?

* * *

A thick silence settles over the room. The figure of Death hovers over it, sneering for eternity at biases, prejudices, and hatreds.

A thick silence settles in, akin to the deafening quiet of a world that has ended, under an extinct sun...in the future...when Jews and non-Jews will become one single dust.

But Mazaltob's uncle, who cannot remain silent for long, notes with slight irony:

"My dear Jean, high up on Sirius where you live, it is easy to judge when looking down on religion."

"What are you waiting for to choose one?" Mazaltob suddenly and vehemently interrupts. "Once, five years ago, you made me think that you would come around to our God..."

"Five years ago, Mazaltob, I also told you that no religion was beautiful to me. At the time, however, that declaration was far from having in my mouth the same meaning it has today when I reiterate it..."

"Yes, I know," sighs Jean, "I will need courage to walk away from the beautiful sunray casting light upon me...We look down upon all those who take an unconventional path. And because I rejected a ready-made God, and I slowly recreated Him in my brain and in my heart, because my God is a cosmic God who juggles both nebulae and suns. He gives to the Earth—that chunk of mud—no greater importance than it has, and finally, because He soars over vengeance and over hatred—for all those reasons, I shall march, solitary, amongst all men, perhaps exiled even from love..."

A deep hush fell once again upon the room: kind in Léa, attentive in Serge, somewhat tense in Salomon, and sorrowful in Mazaltob.

Gazing at his beloved, Jean lowers his eyes, bending his shoulders as if suddenly carrying an invisible cross.

* * *

"I wish, my son," Dr. Bralakoff says to Jean, "to visit my Russia once again. Our good Tetouanis are by now as used to Serge as they are to me...I intend to depart soon. Why not come with me? Nothing keeps you here.

"After that pilgrimage to my native land, we could settle in France. We would, if you'd like, go to one of those small provincial towns that are so peaceful the past whispers in your ears. With your father's inheritance, you could leisurely dedicate yourself to your artistic tastes, and perhaps shine in the arts, in literature, or in music. And then, you ought to marry, son, for it is no secret that celibacy is not in the long term healthy for you. You need a cushiony life, padded in that calm tenderness only found in the home, next to a loving spouse. Who knows? You might even meet another Léa in France!"

But Jean stays quiet.

So, the doctor, vaguely intuiting, adds:

"You mustn't stay in this town, son. No, you must not."

* * *

It's Saturday afternoon.

Jean, hoping at last to find Mazaltob alone, has returned once again to the Macíases' home. But as soon as he crosses the doorstep, the children—shouting: "Show us! Show us!"—attack him.

And every head, even Mazaltob's head, instantly leans over his sketchbook. They are fighting to look at the drawings.

"There, here is Samuelito…"

"That's exactly him… But he looks like he is waiting for something…"

"The hour of the Neïlah,[3] perhaps!"

"And look at Séty, even her beauty mark is there!"

"You mean her ugliness mark," replies Abramito, teasing.

"Aren't you mean!" retorts Séty, furious. "May a sated lion eat you alive!"

"I see," says Eliahou, leaning closer to Jean, "that you have highlighted the vertical groove going from the nose to the upper lip just as it is in reality."

"Why do we have that indentation?" asks the interested party, unabashedly staring at himself.

"Well," explains old David, who for some time now has joined his children, "an angel struck that spot too hard."

"What angel?" asks little Mossé, who has a bit of a lisp.

"The angel who presides over our birth," confirms old David solemnly. "Children are in Eden before being called to this world. Do you know they could reveal many a beauteous thing from that world above us? But an angel is watching.

"As soon as a baby ventures the tip of his tiny nose down here on earth, the angel taps his wand on the baby's lips to keep him quiet.

"Of that stroke of the wand, we've all kept the trace," concludes old Macías quite earnestly.

Mazaltob can't help turning to Jean with a smile that says: "How naïve they are!" A smile from Mazaltob… finally!

The young man is beaming.

Jean, forgetting his sadness and his doubts, listens to the voice within him singing a Hallelujah.

* * *

Lately, Léa has been quite lethargic.

The pink on her cheeks is not as pink, and her eyes have less of a sparkle.

"She needs a change of air," says Doctor Bralakoff.

"That's easy," replies Serge. "One of my friends owns a villa near Gibraltar. We could rent it for three months since he will be in England for the summer."

"I would be happy to, if you come with me," says Léa to her husband.

"That's impossible, darling...unless my patients decide to go on strike. But father and Jean could get you settled. And you could take with you your devoted servant Rachel."

"No. I will die of boredom."

"I could come to spend the Sabbath with you."

"Listen, sister-in-law," says Jean, "I could visit once in a while, as I must meet one of my friends in the South of Spain."

"No. No. No."

"You're not thinking of enduring the summer in that overheated Judería, are you?"

"Yes," replies Léa, pursing her lips like a child, "I will stay here and make every effort to get sick in order to punish you for abandoning me."

"My darling..." begins Serge.

"Wait," interrupts Bralakoff. "I am sure that we could find her a companion among our young Tetouani girls, who are so lacking in distractions."

* * *

From the back of the small steamship, Ceuta shrinks from view. Across the fiery strait, the Rock looms, impressively, its city clinging to it like a leech.

An androgynous dusk descends on the harbor as boats twinkle with lanterns. The moon's crescent becomes snarled in the ropes of the masts.

On each side, the lighthouses of Europe and of Africa exchange sharp glances across the Strait. We can hear a small boat in the distance, its cadenced noise fading away in the night.

The Rock is getting closer. We can finally make out the mouths of the cannons: Gibraltar.

* * *

It's early in the evening, the hour when silence and solitude suddenly permeate every particle of space.

Mazaltob, leaning on the ship's rail next to Léa, breathes in deeply the hour's serenity.

Mazaltob

Her first freedom! Her first trip! And above all, her first encounter with Europe!

This is an almost-African Europe that she will likely never explore further...But it is also Spain, the sacred repository of her ancestors' dulling bones.

Mazaltob is deeply moved. She feels that back in Ceuta, which is still visible in the mists of dusk, she peeled off a layer, the one which she must don each day as "woman of Tetouan," and that another Mazaltob, the Mazaltob of French culture from the school of the Alliance, the Mazaltob who sang operatic arias with Madame Gérard, Jean's Mazaltob—that Mazaltob has now forever engulfed her.

Ah! Never to think again of the Judería and of all the grief from the last few weeks: Her father's marriage to Sol, a few months ago, and Sol's envy of her beauty, for which Sol will not forgive her! Is Sol that ugly? Yes. Worse, even: no sooner have we looked at her face than we've already forgotten it.

* * *

Sol's hostility, a woman's petty hatred, a sly hatred which pierces like safety pins. The old maid was promoted, through her marriage to David, to lady of the house; Mazaltob, now her subordinate, must obey.

Terse commands that hurt more for the manner in which they are uttered than for what they express. Cruel words said casually, with a sarcasm that makes you clench your fists...Sol approves of nothing Mazaltob does...precisely because it is Mazaltob doing it.

And when Léa, who understood it all, said:

"Darling, could you come to Gibraltar to spend time with me in the villa Serge rented?" Sol, looking at Mazaltob, answered:

"Yes, yes, take her with you."

* * *

The sharp song of a small bird pierces the sky like an arrow. A buzzing bee sneaks in between the shades, while the scent of jasmine bursts through the air in the shifting breeze, popping up again all the way in the bedroom.

Mazaltob feels the morning's glow behind the pink curtain of her eyelids—a morning freshly washed off from the night's sleepiness.

It is so delightful to be at the mercy of each day...

* * *

A ray of sunshine sneaks in through the curtains and, climbing into the bed, starts caressing our sleeping beauty. In the garden downstairs, Léa is singing at the top of her lungs . . . no doubt to awaken her friend.

Mazaltob opens her eyes, smiles, and rises. Her bare feet clonk on the wobbly parquet in a joyful rhythm, joined by the sounds of an old mirrorless armoire and a heavy commode.

Shades squeak:

"Wooooo!"

"Wooooo!"

A pair of black eyes at the window and a pair of blue eyes in the garden exchange tender hellos even before mouths can utter them.

Then:

"Hurry, darling, the tea rose has opened last night!"

"But I am not yet ready . . ."

"No one cares! Only old Rachel and I can see you. And, regardless, your nightdress is perfectly decent."

"Fine, fine, madame: I'll obey."

* * *

Looking from a small gazebo past the road to La Linea, Léa gazes at the blue sea which is covered in a pink frosting.

A ruffling of leaves: Mazaltob has arrived.

Her lovely black hair is falling on her shoulders. Her pure neck shoots up, proud of holding high her head—that splendid flower. One hardly reckons her slender body beneath the countless pleats of the supple fabric of her dress.

And Léa recalls that day in Paris at the Pantheon when, before Puvis de Chavannes's painting of Saint Genoveva, she lingered far too long.

* * *

Gardens filled with fragrances in which, as in a symphony when a note dares to rise higher, a stronger scent suddenly dominates!

Gardens, filled with myriad flowers: roses with a hidden heart, lilacs purpureal as the Milky Way, lilies with velvety pistils, geraniums crisp as a child's cheeks!

Tree crowns resembling green nebulae, their infinitude tamed by the curvature of a leaf! Butterflies in wedding frocks; butterflies in full regalia! Scissortail birds slashing the air striated by swarming bees.

Gardens, miniature Edens, the fervent soul of a woman kneels before you.

* * *

Far from the Judería and its strangled horizons, Mazaltob counts her life's blessings. There is the morning in Kitane—already eight years ago—and today's morning. And then there are nights, too: the night in Rio Martine—so sweet that the sea voluptuously shivered in the moonlight—and that other night pulsating with only one kiss...

* * *

They would have liked to visit the town. They went up the hill of Calle Real, mused under the trees of the public park, and paid a visit to the small English cemetery, in which graves are embellished with geraniums as red as the British flag.

They would have liked to visit the town... but here is the catch: they are just two women on their own. One is too pretty, the other too beautiful. And the admiration of men erupts at each of their steps, gushing forth abruptly and, sometimes, too graphically.

If Spaniards are hotheaded, their hearts burn even faster. "*Bendita sea la madre que te parió*"[4] they shout to Mazaltob's face. Some of them, following an old-fashioned custom from their country, even throw a cape at the young lady's feet, so that she will walk on it.

But while Léa can hardly hold back her laughter, which at once causes her lip to purse, her dark-haired friend stiffens and blushes, evidently embarrassed and uneasy.

"Oh darling!" observes the Alsatian girl, "why is it that no one sings 'l'Internationale' of Beauty and its influence on the rapprochement of nations? These descendants of Torquemada admire you, unaware that you are Jewish. But were they to know it, they would adore you no less, because a lovely pair of eyes is more powerful than all the creeds of hatred."

But ever since, Mazaltob refuses to leave the villa.

* * *

She is wearing a simple straight white dress with a high neckline à la *vierge* and sleeves to the elbows. It is a charming dress, very plain and simple, a dress that Mazaltob sewed, with Léa's help, in two afternoons.

As soon as the young woman tries it on, her blonde Alsatian friend pins a red rose to the bodice.

"It's like blood over snow," says Mazaltob.

"An ardent soul beneath a snow-white face," replies Léa, adding:

"Do you know how pretty you look? How beautiful he will think you!"

"Who is he?"

"The One who comes into every woman's life one day!"

And Mazaltob, with a poor smile, whispers:

"He has already come to mine, Léa, but he has left for Argentina."

"Oh, darling!" replies Serge's wife with a mischievous wink, "that's not who I was thinking of..."

* * *

"Mazaltob, before I meet my friend in Algeciras, I have stopped off in Gibraltar to speak with you. But I only have three words to say to you, and here they are: I love you...

"Oh, please, don't walk away! What do you fear, my angel? I have been yours for a long time, perhaps even since that evening when you returned from Kitane—so white and yet with eyes so dark. You were so moved after seeing spring at close range... And then I left, thinking that, behind me in Tetouan, remained only a beloved sister... But when I saw your eyes again, I understood. Yes, I understood, oh Mazaltob, that I must gaze at your eyes as long as I am living, and once dead, know the pious touch of your hands over my body.

"Mazaltob, you, who, deep in my heart, I already call my wife. Mazaltob, I have said too much when only three words suffice: I love you."

Mazaltob gives no answer. Holding onto the gazebo's railing, she gazes in the distance at the ocean festooned with seafoam.

Amidst myriad small noises of the garden close-by and the palpitating ocean, a halo of silence circles her. A halo of silence in which she thinks she can hear Jean's heartbeat...

Mazaltob

Mazaltob is mute. What has happened to her soul?

Jean, trying to find out, takes his friend's head in his hands and turns it toward him: her dark eyes are awash in tears.

"Mazaltob, pretty Mazaltob, do you cry of joy or of sadness?"

Mazaltob stammers, her voice cracked from sobbing so much:

"I cry of sadness, Jean, because I know that you will suffer..."

"Mazaltob..."

"Because the truth is that I love you as I did when I was a child... I love you as a brother for whom one has too much love, but still as a brother."

"Mazaltob, you're lying," goes on Jean, now more forcefully. "You took off your headscarf the night before my arrival. And I know that when, on a stormy night, you shed a tear on my forehead, it wasn't a dream."

"Jean, there is a hint of vanity in the heart of every woman. There is also a great deal of pity..."

Léa's sunny voice suddenly bursts in through the foliage.

"Mazaltob! Jean! Are we having lunch at dinnertime today?"

* * *

After a short stay in Algeciras, Jean would like to show his friend Gibraltar. How he sighed with relief when his companion fell for his amorous ruse!

"Léa, Mazaltob, I'd like you to meet Mr. Charles Balder, the most Jewish of my friends."

"And the most Catholic, too," adds Charles Balder, bowing.

"I like that, monsieur," says Serge's wife, holding out her small hand to the young man. "I am fond of eccentric types."

"You are very kind, madam, but I assure you that where you see quirkiness, it is, instead, mere reflection. Indeed, it is reflection which allows me to shun the prejudices of some of my coreligionists. To be antisemitic is to be more Catholic than the Pope. Was God—the God adored by Christians, who chose a Jewish woman to be his son's mother—an antisemite? There were plenty of other women—Romans, for instance—on Earth."

"That is precisely what most will not forgive us: that the son of God came from our people."

"Yes," adds Charles Balder, "perhaps that's what it means to be the chosen people... But alas, you are now paying dearly for the honor of having in your veins the same blood as Christ."

"Ah, monsieur," says Léa, "too few remember, as you do, that Jesus was himself a Semite. And yet, born of a Jewish woman, in a Jewish land and in a Jewish milieu, your Lord never rejected his Hebrew brethren. Wasn't he circumcised, as they had been, eight days after his birth? Didn't he grow up among them, speaking only their language and studying their Law?"

"Yes," continues Charles Balder, "he assiduously attended the Jewish temple from which he one day expelled the merchants, and nobody was more devout than he. Joseph, his putative father, respected Judaism's most minute religious practices, and I am sure that the Virgin Mary did not work on Saturdays. Later when the Nazarene was older, it was not amidst the Romans, but amidst the Jews that he chose the twelve disciples—one for each tribe of Israel—who later became the Apostles. And when, haloed in goodness, he began spreading the word of God, he spoke Aramaic, which is closely related not to Latin, but to Hebrew.

"That is something that I, as a practicing Catholic, cannot forget, which is why the love I have for Our Lord is a little bit reflected on the people from which He comes.

"Jesus! . . . He embodies all the goodness, all the human kindness! So deep was his love of humankind, that he died of it. Jesus, my soul is filled with Him, and when, disregarding the legend which portrays him as blonde, I imagine him instead with brown curls and the olive complexion of the children of Judea, I imagine that, on the Cross, this is what He said of you: 'Forgive them, God, for they know not what they do!'"[5]

"Ah! Indeed, he was right! The Jews had no idea what they were doing."

"This is why they deserved to be forgiven! If someone today said that he was of divine origin, would you believe him? A God with whom we rub shoulders every day, a God who, like a mere mortal, we watch eat and drink, that God would hardly rouse many followers . . ."

"That is indeed true. Jesus himself understood this when he said: 'No one is a prophet in his own land.' Ah! Had he preached in lands other than Palestine, perhaps there would have been no Calvary for which to hold us responsible. Israel's great sin, as it happens, was modesty in excess: Poor Jews who could not fathom God as their brother! Therein lies what separates our religions, sisters nevertheless in their beginnings . . ."

"Sisters to this day, despite the wickedness of men. Isn't the Bible the foundation of both? The commandments found in the Christian catechisms are precisely those Moses once inscribed on the Tablets of the Law, and Jesus preserved in the new religion the Hebrew custom of burying the dead by contrast with the practice amidst Roman pagans of incinerating them. In the end, you see, Christianity is nothing other than Judaism revisited by the ingenuity of Christ."

Turning toward his friend, Charles Balder concludes:

"Jean, you who are the son of Japheth and of Shem, you of mixed race and with equal bonds to both religions, you assuredly will not dispute me."

No, Jean, the fierce debater, Jean the free thinker, will not dispute his friend: he heard nothing. And that's because in the eyes of Mazaltob, who is lost in a distant dream, he tries to lay hold of her elusive soul... elusive as if against her will.

* * *

The gentle swaying of palm leaves punctuates the silvery silence of the night. Under the amorous moon, they walk solemnly as if in a dream. As they emerge from the thick vegetation of the alleys, they see the star-studded heavens anew in their glory.

The two of them stand alone. Alone with the light breeze rustling through the leaves. They are quiet.

Meanwhile, a cloud coming from the ocean wanders through the sky and Jean, in the half-penumbra which now conceals his face, finally dares to speak:

"Mazaltob, Mazaltob... I am sure what you say is a lie, just as I am sure of my love..."

"Jean..."

"Mazaltob, you love me. Your lips may say something else, but I have read it in your eyes."

"I have already told you, Jean: You're nothing more than a brother to me."

"Shush, this is too painful! Mazaltob, you who are my religion, does my irreligion frighten you?"

"No, Jean. Despite my desire to see you as one of us, I believe the Eternal cherishes kindness above all, even coming from a non-believer."

"Is it disbelief to worship outside of conventional norms?"

"Oh, brother, you have your own way of loving God. And since to love your way is plenty, I will not be one to blame you for it!"

"Do not, my love, insult me with a name against which your heart, like mine, rebels. Is it my Aryan blood, the blood of the Inquisitors from Spain, that repels you?"

"The Inquisitors? 'God, forgive them, they knew not what they did!'"

"Thank you, my precious, you are so true to my ideal that I dare not ask: Is it perhaps because I am not Sephardi?"

"The God of Israel calls all of Abraham's children, without exception, his."

"Mazaltob, I knew too well your beautiful soul to ever doubt your answers. Mazaltob, my love, you must find lying painful. Let word of my happiness flower on your lips..."

* * *

In the darkness, Jean takes her trembling hand and just like on that other night he lays an endless kiss on it.

In between the clouds suspended like open curtains, the moon reappears to preside over the garden. Atop the gazebo, the two young people are now sitting on a bench. The gentle breeze brings them, mingled with the intermittent sea scent, the nearby perfume of jubilant jasmines. In this blissful night, Mazaltob answers:

"I will tell you the truth, Jean, but you must promise me something."

Jean quivers with joy as he fancies his future happiness in the eyes and the voice of his friend.

"Mazaltob, my life, I hereby swear to you that your will is my command."

"You must remember your words. You have now made a promise. And now, listen since you've wished for it: I, too, my Jean, love you with all my soul, with all my being..."

"Mazaltob... my beloved... my wife..."

"Your wife? Alas, no, I belong to another!"

"Your husband's desertion should set you free, my love."

"My husband! I will not forget my duties where he has forgotten his! I believe that only death revokes a marriage blessed by Adonaï."

"Mazaltob... are you serious? How could you think your God so demanding, you who are so broad-minded to permit the worship of other gods?"

"If even I can't understand myself, how could you? Alas! Inside of me is a 'woman of Tetouan' who cannot be destroyed!"

"And now you must remember your promise. You must leave for good..."

"Enough, have mercy...You've shattered me. But no, that cannot be true, you must be testing me, right?"

Placing her lips on the forehead of the young man, who swoons at once with bliss and with agony, Mazaltob, filled with sorrow, whispers between sobs:

"Obey me...and forgive me, my love."

Chapter 11

Three years have passed.

Jean and Doctor Bralakoff live in France, in "one of those small provincial towns which are so peaceful that the past whispers in your ears."

As for Mazaltob, forced to leave the parental home due to the merciless jealousy of her stepmother, she now lives with Preciada.

José Jalfon's wife, Jean's admirer, is still very beautiful, but at only twenty-one, there is something lifeless and despondent on her face which, even more than her erstwhile splendid beauty, hooks the eye and will not let go.

Memories, the ceaseless grindstone of the soul!

Memories, you are Mazaltob's greatest bliss and her greatest torment. Dream of love, you fall from the pinnacle and shatter, all in vain...

Yet, cruel, you never die.

The young woman now loathes living under the Judería's narrow sky. Closing her eyes, she imagines every so often what her life might have been with Jean "elsewhere." She fancies, somewhere in that France she once learned to love in her schoolbooks, a villa even more lovely than the one in Gibraltar, because a more amiable sky rests atop its roof. They are strolling along the alleys, holding each other by the waist. Jean speaks in a warm and collected voice. He then grows quiet... and his gaze, turned toward his beloved, still says: "I love you..."

But comes nighttime... All around them the garden opens depths of velvet, filled with tantalizing perfumes...

And their faces grow closer because they can no longer see each other...

Jean...

Does she regret banishing him from her life? Yes. For there is no duty against which youth does not eventually grow rebellious.

Mazaltob

Duty!... Inside Mazaltob's aching brain, the word rolls to and fro, tinkling ceaselessly like a lead ball inside a metal sphere. What does it mean "to do your duty"? It means to sacrifice yourself for someone else's happiness. It means to trample, if you must, your own heart, and to offer it as a bloody holocaust to someone you love. But how hollow the word rings when it is intended for José Jalfon, who was perhaps brazen enough to have rebuilt his home in Argentina!

"You have your God," says Mazaltob's alter ego—"the woman from Tetouan." And Mazaltob replies:

"No."

And that's because, seeking to assuage the wound of her self-sacrifice during those three painful years, she read and reread the Old Testament. As a result, that terrible and prejudiced God she adored in childhood gradually withdrew from her, fading away into Infinity...

A new God slowly replaced it, each day winning the ground lost by the other; He's a God busy with proclaiming the silent glory of the sun in the sky, not with vengeances or with battles—a poet-God who distills in each droplet of dew a particle of the dawn which makes it glow.

A great God. A logical God because, having created all men—the white, the black, the yellow, and the red—He loves them all equally...

Because His purpose is not to grant our planet—that shred of dirt lost in the ether—greater importance than it actually has...

It is a cosmic God who juggles both nebulae and stars... It is Jean's God.

"Why have I scorned happiness?" wonders Mazaltob ever so often. "Who would have wept if I had listened to my heart and had become the wife of my childhood companion? My mother is dead. In my father's life, rife with the screams of my stepmother, there is little room for me.

"Preciada? Her children, her husband, and her household, all are a buffer between us. Uncle Salomon? My aunts? My cousins? They are old: the ground is already opening beneath their feet... They would have had little opportunity to curse me...

"Alas! No one required that vain sacrifice of me, and you, Jean, who has hauled your moribund life across the ocean, Jean, will you ever forgive me, my light?"

Blanche Bendahan

* * *

Fortuitous events so seldom occur in the life of a woman from Tetouan! Days roll by in a single line, each similar to the previous one, only undone by Marriage, Birth, and Death.

In the Jewish cemetery, there is now a new grave next to the grave of Mrs. Macías: alas! For a year now, little Mossé, Mazaltob's younger brother, has been "resting" there.

Not a single one of Tetouan's seven thousand Jews will ever forget the circumstances of his death! Not one!

* * *

On that day, the Arab quarter was in commotion: it was the 'Idal-Kabir.

It is customary on that holiday to slaughter a sheep in the presence of the Caliph. The slaughterer, however, needs to ensure that the knife used to cut the animal's throat does not kill it at once. For there is a long way from the Caliph's palace to the great Mosque, and the animal must make it still panting! Otherwise, all Muslims believe it will be a drought year.

Thus, the Caliph's emissary, riding on that day at full gallop, carried on his saddle the wretched sheep in the throes of death.

May Allah grant us a timely arrival in the sanctuary, which must collect the animal's last breath in order to secure an abundant harvest!

Fearing the anger of his master were he to arrive too late to his destination, the horseman, drunk with speed, spurred on his horse. Arabs and Jews alike, knowing that nothing could stop the implacable thrust of the horse racing at breakneck speed, hastily moved aside to make way for him.

At that very moment, little Mossé happened to be in the *Morería*, the Arab quarter, where Old David, like many Jews, kept shop.

The child was playing on one of its streets—which are as narrow as those of the Judería—when the horseman and his bloody sheep emerged from a dark archway. The rider could see from afar the breathing obstacle standing in his way but, blinded by the mission to be accomplished, did not moderate his speed. Too bad for that foolish little Jew! Allah's will must not wait!

And before the witnesses of this scene could even attempt to rescue the boy, the horse charged the panic-stricken baby, and the animal's

100

heavy horseshoes pierced the child's delicate chest. Indifferent to the lamentations, the threats, and the clenched fists of the crowd, deaf like fate, blind like death, the horseman had already disappeared into one of the small streets.

Shortly after, the Jews, aggrieved and angered, poured into the Morería, sacking the shops and manhandling the Arabs, who threw stones at them in retaliation. That day is known ever since as "the Day of Stones."[1]

Poor little Mossé! Mazaltob used to sing to him one of those old Spanish ballads when she tucked him in at night. And when his first tooth came in three years ago, she made him the traditional porridge made with wheat and chickpeas called *lentina*.

We, Jews, do not mourn the death of a child—that angel which a merciful God took away before he could sin.

But is this grief, added to countless others, that which renders Mazaltob's cheeks whiter than a statue's marble?

*   *   *

Nonetheless, there isn't only sorrow for the Macías family; there are joys, too. Preciada is now a mother to twin boys.

Twins! And boys! That's a woman's insurance policy for instant admittance to Heaven . . . eventually. Because the Eternal blesses she who gives birth to two boys in one day. That feat bestows indeed such great fame upon the woman it is as though she had something to do with it.

Preciada is jubilant. She has "graduated" now.

And despite her appearance, further to her detriment—her small eyes, now looking all the more like tiny nits, her sagging breasts, signs of an already vanishing youth, her hips wide as a barge swaying with each move—she would not trade her fate with anyone.

Her real life began the moment when, freed at last from the pains of childbirth, she beheld the wrinkly faces of her two small *varones*.[2]

Not only does she no longer complain but, much like the pious man upon beginning to read a new prayer book, she would readily write on the first page of her new life:

"Bessimana Taba."[3]

As for Mazaltob, despite her name, which scorns adversity, she hasn't been very lucky, poor girl! That's because there is no room in Preciada's tiny brain for the idea that her sister's fate could change. For if men have little control over their own life, women have even less.

Happiness? God gives it and God takes it away. And as Job said when he sat on his dung heap: Blessed be the Eternal's name.

*   *   *

To elude her melancholy, Mazaltob tries to be as useful as possible in her elder sister's home. "She is very devoted and, as our local saying goes," says her brother-in-law—the twins' father, "I love her like an old slipper."

The wife of José Jalfon is indeed very devoted! Needle and scissors in hand, she dresses everyone in the house from head to toe. She supervises the preparation of the household's jams and preserves. Preciada is too preoccupied with her daughter and her two sons!

Every so often, when she sees the beautiful reflection of her overly white face on the coppery surface of a maslin pan, hope creeps in the heart of the young woman. Indeed, hope springs eternal when one is young!

"Dare not speak ill of daylight as long as it's not yet dark out," she heard her parents say. While there is still a breath of life in us, only God knows what the future has in store.

Perhaps Jean will come back...

And that charming friend who, like him, has blue eyes and translucent skin, perhaps she'll be back, too...

Oh, Léa! Blonde daughter of the North who would not acclimate to Africa, physically or spiritually! Léa, you have returned to the storks of your childhood roofs!

A Jewish doctor no longer cares for the people of the Judería. That loving couple who strolled arm-in-arm down its streets causing amazement, has now left and is faraway.

*   *   *

Nevertheless, a white envelope with a French stamp brightens Mazaltob's dark life once in a while: Jean's sister-in-law has not forgotten her.

Those letters! They cause such turmoil in the soul of the lovely Israelite! First because they speak of Jean, then for the dreaded advice they bestow.

In our brief existence—they say—joy only reveals itself to those fighting to conquer it. Women, like men, are born free under the sky. There are saintly duties we must not escape, but there are others which, beneath their pageantry, mask only prejudice. You must live your life. Because of Mazaltob, Jean is dying of sorrow. Because of herself, Mazaltob is dying, too.

But this time, the sole confidante of David's daughter adds one more thing.

"Do not resort to a religious pretext. You must indeed know that the *get*—this permission to remarry granted by a divorcé to his soon-to-be ex-wife—was precisely devised to dissolve a marriage.

"Your José Jalfon to whom you feel so tied, why not search for him in Buenos Aires and ask him for the blessed document that would set you free? Having abandoned you, your man must surely care little if you rebuild your life.

"Come on, hurry, hurry, my sweet friend. Every wasted minute is an emolument to nothingness. Hurry to seize happiness: the narrow graves awaiting us only have room for one chastened gesture: to cross your hands on your chest."

* * *

"I wish to see Mrs. Jalfon."

Sewing by the small window of her room, Mazaltob suddenly startles, her heart racing. What could that voice, which she recognizes without putting a face on it, want from her? Is it happiness or sorrow which, through that opening door downstairs, will be ushered into her life? But Preciada's strident call pierces the air:

"Mazaltob! Mazaltob! Someone is here for you."

Mazaltob comes down hastily. In the sitting room to which the guest is ceremoniously escorted, she catches a glimpse of Charles Balder.

What does Jean's friend say to her? She remembers nothing. Oh yes . . . he says that he came to study the city's customs for his book. He says that Jean told her once about this strange Judería, which one either likes or dislikes, but which will not leave you indifferent . . . He says that amidst the world's uniform march of progress, there is a city which is still redolent of the Middle Ages, and that city is Tetouan . . .

What else does he say to her? She only finds out when Preciada leaves

103

them alone to prepare the pastries which every well-mannered Tetouani woman ought to serve.

Then, almost in a whisper, he discloses the spiritual distress of his friend. Jean's life, he says, has been shattered. He now wanders through the silent streets of a French town, impervious to all, he who vibrated like a harp before the bluest horizon. Art itself has shut before him the sacred gate of its sanctuary, and Poetry has swiftly moved away from the only soul scorning her...

Only terrible chest pains awake every so often this living-dead that Jean has become, and then, Mazaltob's childhood companion speaks of her by turns as his sun or as his executioner: "I do not have much time left to obey you, my darling," he screams, between sobs. "Death will soon relieve me of the burden of my promise!"

"Madame," concluded Charles Balder somberly, "whatever your motivations are, I will only say one more thing: Mercy!"

Chapter 12

"It's because of me his life is shattered... Because of me!"

And Mazaltob curses herself. Why did she banish Jean? Why did she fight her desire to see him again? What fallacious grasp of the word "duty" gave her the right to make someone suffer?

* * *

"Nevertheless, you did the right thing," approves the sectarian God of her childhood. "Jean doesn't believe in me."

"No, you have sinned," counters the other God, the God of logic who loves all His children equally, be they Christian, Jewish, or simply deistic, that God who loves even the atheist...

* * *

Oh! And to say that, had she willed it, there would be on this earth a soul filled with joy, a heart enthralled by another one beating next to it!

And she could have known happiness, her very own happiness, before the indifferent stillness of the grave... Had she willed it...

But who ordered the veto which ruled over the tender aspirations of a young woman for so long? A victorious day has been shining for some time over her secretly expanded religion, one in which reason holds sway. Yet, doesn't she remain hardened against herself despite her transformation?

* * *

Mazaltob descends into her soul's depths and plumbs them ceaselessly, her thoughts groping, reaching out for each argument as if to the jagged edges of a rock. Oh, how much she would like to know! How much she would like to understand!

Suddenly, the beautiful Jewish girl lifts up her head as though "Eureka!" had been whispered into her ears. She knows.

She knows that the Mazaltob scorning happiness isn't she. Neither is it the one who read novels, or the one who listened, entranced, to Kitane's glorious morning symphony. Nor is it the one who nearly fainted, bewitched by the night of Rio Martine, or that other one whose passionate voice used to sing opera at Madame Gérard's . . . And finally, it's not, either, the Mazaltob on a school bench, who heard the rhythms of exquisite French verse pulsating within her . . .

Indeed, now she knows that the one who rebelled against Love is the other Mazaltob, the "woman from Tetouan," the one held captive by the Judería, not physically, but spiritually. She knows that an atavistic loyalty weighs upon that woman, that the blood of her distant foremothers stoned for adultery courses through her veins.

It is the "woman from Tetouan" whose flesh only wants to know one man.

It is the "woman from Tetouan" who has only one man in her life.

*   *   *

Salomon guides Charles Balder through the Judería's maze, so perplexing to foreigners.

And Jean's friend is enthralled with his tour guide who, in addition to his native Spanish, "gets by" in French, Arabic, and even English . . .

Besides, Mazaltob's uncle knows every legend of the country, as well as the original "reason" for the most eccentric customs—a knowledge that comes in handy!

But the tales of our Don Quixote from Tetouan are less biased than one would expect, no doubt because in this Jewish patriot chauvinism—this enemy of well-being—has no place.

*   *   *

It's pouring today, and the two men meet in Preciada's patio to chat.

From her room nearby, Mazaltob, sewing, listens.

"Tell me a story from Tetouan, Monsieur Salomon," asks Charles Balder.

"Well, you already know my entire repertory . . ."

"Oh, please, please . . . No excuses . . . I know you have a saying which claims that 'Kind words will unlock iron doors.' So, I beg you gently . . ."

"Fine, I will tell you the story of the closed 'mem.'"

"Very well. But first, what is a 'mem'?"

"It is a Hebrew letter, the fourteenth in our alphabet. It has no end and no beginning, just like the letter 'O' in the Roman alphabet: it is closed from all ends. Listen:

"A long time ago—I was perhaps fifteen—one of those great sages that we call hahamim, and one of the most clever men I knew, was a judge in a rabbinical court. So clever indeed that those Jews with disagreements purposely came to see him. One day a Jew named Samuel came before Rabbi Jacob—thus shall my hero be called—and spoke in the following manner:

"'I once had a cauldron filled with gold coins. Before leaving on a trip, I asked my neighbor, Joseph, to keep it until I returned. "Listen," he replied, "I know a place to safely bury your treasure." So, on a moonless night, we set out for the countryside faraway, and we buried the treasured cauldron at the foot of a fig tree. I was gone for a month. Upon my return, I asked my neighbor for my possession. Wo! He pretended not to know! I went to the tree . . . I dug the earth . . . The hiding place was empty. . . Yes, empty, Oh Rabbi, may lightning strike me if I am lying!'

"'Do you have proof of this theft, you foolish and gullible man?'

"'None.'

"'All right.'

"The wise Rabbi summoned Joseph, the defendant, who was promptly brought before him. But it was a whole other matter to have him confess his misdeed! And if it were not a question of Jews, I would say the tribunal struggled with what saint to turn to that day! All of a sudden, however, Rabbi Jacob seemed to have an idea:

"'Are you sure,' he said to Samuel, 'that nobody saw you burying the cauldron?'

"'There was,' said the defendant, 'God who sees everything, my neighbor, myself, and the fig tree in between whose roots we laid down the treasure.'

"'All right. Please fetch me a leaf from that fig tree.'

"When Samuel left, Rabbi Jacob summoned Joseph, and inquired about his children and his wife. Then, as though he had been able to visit Joseph's farm in between prayers, he discussed vine, grain, and even cattle.

He spoke softly and gently, this Rabbi Jacob, who was so damn smart, that no one in the audience harbored any misgiving on the verdict about to be returned. As for the accused, Joseph, he had no doubt, either, on the felicitous outcome of his trial. So, while Joseph confidently answered the rabbi's questions, the rabbi suddenly leaned toward him and said, loud enough to be heard by everyone:

"'Oh, and regarding that cauldron of yours, son, continue to keep your mouth shut like the letter "mem."'

"To which Joseph, trusting, foolishly answered:

"'That is precisely what I am doing, Rabbi!' Thus our clever haham learned the truth."

* * *

From her room nearby, Mazaltob listens, attentive and amused in spite of herself. And as darkness falls, the Judería seizes her again by the shoulder.

* * *

But she will put up a fight. She will break free from this Judería, with its vice-like walls that constrict her heart and push against the sky.

She will leave with Jean, far…very far…to finally sing the impassioned poem fancied in adolescence, that lovely poem filled with passion that Tetouan has never learned…

And, as Léa writes, she will live her life.

By the way, what does it mean exactly, to live one's life? Never had such words been uttered in the Judería…

* * *

At odds with countless heroines from the novels who must wrestle with evil instincts, the wife of José Jalfon, instead, must crush the ancestral inclination for chastity within her.

Her heart's happiness comes at such a price.

* * *

Mazaltob is weary of being trapped inside of herself.

If Madame Gérard were here…If Léa were here…

Alas! There is only Preciada, and although she is kind-hearted, passion is for her what light is for someone born blind.

Mazaltob

Nevertheless, Mazaltob can no longer carry alone the burden of her troubled soul . . . She will seek advice from her older sister. But Preciada is so busy!

It's the change of seasons. Shouldn't we fear the *técoufa*?

The técoufa is an ailment which seizes your head and your stomach, oppresses your chest, and sends your blood shooting up your cheeks all the while running an invisible ice cube down your back.

It afflicts Jewish women who cannot deprive themselves of water on certain days of the year. This is purportedly because after God created angels, He entrusted them with keeping watch over the waters. But the task is so taxing that the celestial creatures take turns: There is a different cherub on sentry duty every three months. The Devil, however, will not relinquish His rights.

During the change of guard, He takes advantage of a momentary lapse of attention, in which the outgoing sentry is instructing the incoming one to cast a bloody tide which adulterates the waters at the source.

There is a second explanation that contends that the pollution is caused by the angel of Death upon washing his knife in the pool every three months.

And there is a third one that asserts that the stream of blood is from Seila, daughter of Jephthah the Gileadite, who died to carry out her father's reckless wish.

Finally, there is a fourth version, which argues that the impure stream originates from the Nile, when Moses changed that river to blood.

But since one can make accommodations with every clergy, the técoufa can be avoided if one takes care to place a piece of iron in the water containers. The hard metal acts in this case as an antiseptic.

* * *

Preciada, as we said, is extremely busy. She comes and goes, she lifts every lid, moves every piece of pottery, sticks her nose inside every jar, every bucket, every basin, probing with her small round eyes the depths of every earthenware pot, of every piece of porcelain, of every stoneware jug.

Therefore, Mazaltob will say nothing.

* * *

"How could you not recognize him, my child?" says Uncle Salomon. "It's Josué Aboudaram, from Buenos Aires... Let me situate him for you: Freha's son, the nephew of your late grandmother. Remember now?"

"As for me," the visitor explains, "even after ten years, I would have recognized those peerless dark eyes amidst a thousand others. Oh, I beg you," he adds, gallantly bowing before Mazaltob, "do not blush; I am fifty years old... Alas... lucky me!"

Uncle Salomon guffaws. Always lighthearted, this Josué! Ah! The fellow wears his age lightly on his tongue!

* * *

Meanwhile Preciada, who is a hostess with savoir-vivre, serves delicious sweets named *fijuelas*, which look like spiraling ribbons.

And they chat about Buenos Aires, that lovely capital; they speak of its wide, modern avenues, of its charming Palermo, a sort of South American Bois de Boulogne.

"Do you know my husband, José Jalfon?" Mazaltob suddenly asks.

"Indeed... Though I have long ago lost touch with him."

"What does he do there?"

"Er... Eh... I don't really know," replies Josué Aboudaram, uneasy.

"Oh! I can hear it all," declares Mazaltob, sternly. "I am perfectly aware he has another wife... and also children..."

Josué Aboudaram may be a jovial fellow, but he is not a clever psychologist.

And he is surely a scatterbrain, as he doesn't think for even a minute that Salomon's niece, in telling a lie to get at the truth, employs an eternal feminine strategy.

And carelessly falling into the trap, he explains:

"Indeed, yes... I came across that José Jalfon a few months ago on the Avenida de Mayo..."

He goes on, with sudden exuberance:

"At his arm was an exceptionally pretty lady... Picture this: Parisian chic, hair splashed with gold, mischievous green eyes..."

"Far prettier than those dark eyes you deemed unmatched only a moment ago," concludes Mazaltob with bitter poise.

Josué Aboudaram lowers his head: he realizes he has just blundered.

Mazaltob

"Monsieur Balder...Write Jean to come back."

Charles Balder rises and, deeply moved, shakes Mazaltob's hands.

"Thank you, thank you, Madame...Thank you on behalf of my friend whose life you're saving...Thank you on my behalf for allowing me to soon see him return to life. There, happiness isn't a complicated music, but rather a simple melody: it is useless to overplay the doleful notes to be attuned to its harmony..."

"Yes, I believe we will be happy," replies Mazaltob. "Nevertheless, despite my auspicious first name, I am apprehensive. Apprehensive that I may face a destiny which is silently endured by every woman here...I don't know what strange superstition impels me to desire no other joy than the reluctant kind known in Tetouan..."

"Rest assured, Madame. You are like those statues which an artist gradually chisels out of the thickness of Carrara marble. I can already make out the thrust, the face, and a few body lines. The rest is dormant within the block of marble in which it is imprisoned.

"Your soul soars toward higher spiritual regions, and you have turned your face toward Love. But the gangue of marble still enshrouds you...

"Have courage, please. Keep fashioning yourself. Soon you will break free of the mold: the Judería will no longer detain you."

"Yes," replies the beautiful Jewish woman, lifting her smooth forehead, "I had forgotten to live until now. But for the love of Jean, I will triumph over myself. I must."

Chapter 13

Jean is back.

On seeing him, she wept.

She wept because on his beloved face suffering had painted the most poignant of masks.

And his hands! Those lovely, smooth white hands, those expressive hands. They've become so thin they evoke the bones they shroud.

Ah! May she be cursed!

Others in her place might have swooned with pride to have inspired such love.

How could she have likened herself to those "women from Tetouan" who give themselves for life to the man who takes them as virgins? Those "women from Tetouan" whose children and household forever bind them...

Of marital life Mazaltob knows only painful loathing. She did not cherish those small curly heads which compel a mother to forgive a husband for her most heartbreaking disillusionments...

And how remote from her is that José Jalfon! Remote because of his forty years; remote, too, because of his inclination for vice; remote, finally, because of that irony of his which tears things down but cares not to rebuild them...

And yet, how could she ever forget that she was once his wife and that he tore the seal of her virginal flesh?

Eve remains permanently impregnated with the first man who lay with her; indeed, it is said that children borne of a woman's second marriage resemble not the man who fathered them, but their mother's first husband.

The instinct which compels the "woman from Tetouan" to know only one man—in the Biblical sense of the word—isn't that instinct nature's true voice? A voice, ever powerful, which reawakens just when Civilization believed it silenced?

Isn't it the voice of nature that sneers when a bewildered father seeks in vain his likeness in the face of his newborn child?

* * *

There is not only the one who lays hold of the body, but there's also the one who lays hold of the soul... The one who has forever waited for that female subconscious filled with repressed aspirations.

Men cherish their own gender: women suffer theirs, which for them evokes not joy, but pain. And like a peasant who sings despite his feudal duties, women forget their physical bondage in the dream of an ideal love.

* * *

As for Mazaltob, she dreams of Jean.

* * *

Ah! His heart is the male counterpart to her heart, his brain the male counterpart to her brain! Jean, childhood companion who leaned his angelic face over the books she was reading.

Ah! His crystal-clear eyes in which her own never caught that beastly flash sometimes flickering in José's pupils.

Jean... sweet knight who dreams of no other bliss than a chaste kiss on his damsel's hand.

* * *

There will be in their tenderness lovely ornaments such as flowers, stars, birdsongs, blue nights, and radiant days. There will be wintry nights filled with the poetry he'll read to her in a soft voice... And there will be her singing... and his cello... They will have all those joys of the heart and of the soul, the only ones which do not leave in their wake a long trail of sadness...

* * *

They will have their wondrous love.

* * *

The Judería has no public park with discreet shaded recesses. It has no tearooms, no department stores, no houses with two entrances. The women of the Judería wear neither hat veils nor birdcage veils. They don neither sleeve muffs nor gloves, and they don't even carry a pocketbook in which to slip a billet-doux: the Judería cares not about lovers.

* * *

Nevertheless, this Judería marvels at Jean's unexpected return.

"Why did he come back to Tetouan if the Bralakoffs no longer live here?"

"He came to take notes and to make sketches," say a few young people who, having traveled to Tangier, think they're in the know.

But such a passion for art exceeds the neighborhood's understanding. Others suggest:

He came to meet his friend Charles Balder.

* * *

And although most Tetouani Jews understand friendship far better than they understand art, they think that this trip, though intriguing, is not "Kosher" just the same.

* * *

For Jean to visit Preciada alone is considered harmless: first, because a housewife has no impure thoughts! Second, because everybody knows that the young man visited the Macíases often in the past.

But at the house of Preciada, there is Mazaltob. And if most would find no issue with this—for according to the patriarchal customs of their country, a married woman is immunized against temptation—there is always a jealous someone, someone especially ugly, who insinuates, in between two insignificant words, a malevolent prudishness.

Thankfully, Uncle Salomon and Charles Balder have set up headquarters in Preciada's patio—one of the largest in the Judería—because at old David's home, Sol's ill temper, once she married, is too deafening.

Mazaltob

Chaperoned by two men who shield him from gossip, Jean now only walks through Preciada's doorstep as a threesome.

* * *

They gaze at each other, separated only by the conversation of others, among whom only one knows about their love.

Between them lingers the cloud of Jean's exile, which she still cannot justify to him...

But there is also, despite all their past suffering, a renewed happiness they must hide from all... As well as three years of their own transformations, unknown to the other.

* * *

On this day Salomon brought a rich Arab who is a friend of his: It is useful for someone like Charles Balder, who wishes to learn about the customs of the country, to inquire about such customs from one of the descendants of Ismael, who are so often engaged in the public life of the Jews.

But although Sidi Abdallah speaks very good Spanish, he hasn't learned French. Hence Mazaltob's uncle acts as an interpreter.

"Do you know," he says suddenly, turning toward Jean, "that Sidi Abdallah claims that, of all the days of the week, only Friday, the Muslim day of rest, has been sanctified by God?"

"Such a claim is natural coming from a worshipper of Allah," the young Frenchman ventures with a smile, adding:

"As natural, indeed, as my claim to respect only Sunday..."

"You're mistaken," retorts Salomon, "it's even more natural to consecrate, as I do, only Saturday, which buttresses both Friday and Sunday. Catholics and Mohammedans are both in need of our 'Sabbath.'"

"Oh dear, why argue? On this matter, each must keep his own counsel..."

"Allow me to be right: without the Jewish Sabbath, the Christian Sunday and the Muslim Friday would fall apart. And if you give me two minutes, I will indeed find you proof of this."

Uncle Salomon then goes to the kitchen. He returns shortly thereafter, three small empty jars of equal size in his arms. He puts one of them on the table:

"Here is Saturday," he explains.

Then comes the second container, its rim and part of its belly, despite some balancing problems, resting aslant on the left side of the first container:

"Now here is Sunday."

Uncle Salomon takes the third jar and places it as he did the second, this time resting on the right side of the middle jar:

"And here is Friday."

"Now pay close attention," he declares:

"If I take out Friday, Saturday doesn't fall down. If I take out Sunday, Saturday is still standing.

"But if I remove each of your respective holidays, Saturday remains in place…

"But," adds our Jewish Don Quixote, "follow me: now I lay out the jars as I did earlier, but this time taking Saturday out. Friday and Sunday collapse altogether.

"Although I was joking a moment ago, I meant it quite literally."

"Bravo!" applauds Charles Balder, bemused. "Albeit failing to convert me to your religion, this is an experience I must surely note."

* * *

Although separated by this conversation, Mazaltob and Jean are looking at each other, each far away from the atmosphere which surrounds them.

But Jean is still unaware that beyond the question of which day is holiest, the God Mazaltob worships is his God, too…that cosmic God who juggles both nebulae and suns.

* * *

"My dear Jean," says Charles Balder, "I can't thank you enough for sending me here. Thanks to you, I was able to know Tetouan, capital of the Sephardim, and to follow at close range the life of its Jewish community which a long time ago made its own the following motto: 'One for all, all for one.' Oh, how many false ideas have vanished from my mind!

"Like countless others I believed, for example, that Jews practiced bigamy. The famous passage of Talmudic law allowing Israelites to take two spouses was met with such opprobrium from its critics!

"So immediately upon arrival, I decided to make inquiries precisely on that matter.

"Well, of the seven thousand souls in the Judería, do you know how many bigamous men there are? Only two. And even so, one of them took his second wife only after his first had been pronounced incurably mad.

"What do you think of these Jews who, despite the option to enter a second marriage, choose monogamy, nonetheless? And isn't that monogamy often burdensome to the 'civilized' men of other countries?

"Yes, you were right to send me to Tetouan. I came here just in time: the treaty of Algeciras[1] threatens to change everything around here. A large Spanish postal service will soon replace both the small French postal service and the German one, which are always competing against each other. The old streets of the Judería will be lit up no doubt thanks to electricity. There will be a theater with an usherette whom we tip, and the guttural discussions of the Moors will be punctuated by the bells of intermission from movie theaters.

"But you're not listening, which is why we must, like it or not, get to the subject of your affections."

"My affections?" replies Jean, "will I ever see them blossom?"

"Why, why, aren't you happy?" Charles Balder asks, painfully surprised. "She was the one who asked for your return. You see each other every day..."

"Yes, but have I ever been able to be alone with her for two minutes to tell her that I worship her?" cries Jean feverishly. "Can I whisper to her and not instantly draw the attention of one of hers? Can I escape the central patio from which all eyes continuously scrutinize every room in the house? Yes," he goes on bitterly, "I indeed see her every day. But I know nothing of the spiritual crisis which has shattered her, compelling her to end my exile... I know nothing of the event which freed her from that José Jalfon I abhor... Nevertheless, all that is nothing compared to the fear gnawing at me: you see, I fear that her change of heart might be fictitious; I fear that the Judería might take her back and I in return will have only my grief!"

"My poor friend!" sighs Charles Balder, "when will I experience the satisfaction of seeing you untroubled! This has lasted far too long," he adds, suddenly energized. "From now on, it is I who will be in charge of your happiness. And I swear to you that Mazaltob will soon be your wife."

*   *   *

Today, there is great commotion in the Judería. Daniel Soto, who lived to be one hundred, will be buried in the afternoon.

Daniel Soto was such a pious man! Hence God rewarded him by extending his days to the supreme limit.

He lived for a hundred years! Happy is the elderly person who bears with him this sign of Adonaï's blessing.

The funeral of such a man must differ from all other funerals: we must chant, not the customary funeral lamentations named *kinoth*, but the wedding piyyutim, whose joyous sounds must resonate on the coffin's path.

*   *   *

The notes of the joyous chorus resound all at once. The entire Judería rushes to the terraces of their dwellings, as their windows, square and tiny, won't accommodate more than a few spectators.

Everyone has already deserted Preciada's patio in order to follow their hostess on the steep stairs. The procession comes next. Here are the members of the Hevra Kadisha in their black cloaks, followed by the men from the family of the deceased, and finally by the coffin of Daniel Soto.

At this sight, the women, who are watching from their terraces and their doorsteps, bring their hands to their eyes and their mouth in a sign of respect.

Preciada, too, makes a point of performing that gesture.

But Mazaltob doesn't budge... perhaps because Charles Balder, availing himself of the general inattention around them, is speaking to her in a low, albeit vehement, voice.

*   *   *

That's it, the die is cast! She must leave. Or rather, she must run away...

And she must do it without embracing her father, without embracing her brothers, or her sisters...

She must run away... secretly... like a thief...

How could she face the wrath of the Rabbi who once married her? How could she face the hostility of the Judería, so strict on matters pertaining to the virtue of women?

Mazaltob

Nevertheless, she would have wished to confront her family, holding hands with Jean, and say to them: "Shouldn't you repair the harm you inflicted upon me in marrying me off to one I didn't love? Shouldn't you repair that hurt by allowing me to love Jean?"

But she knows full well that no one in her family would understand such words...

For in the face of religion she is José Jalfon's wife.

But that marriage means nothing before French law, which would bind her to Jean.

And it would be unthinkable to return later to Tetouan without causing a scandal, for the civil law of foreign countries means nothing before the religious Law of Israel.

She will be nothing according to the Judería's disdainful code but a loose woman living with her lover.

Ah, well, what a shame! She has tormented her friend's heart far too long. No matter! She will run away tomorrow.

She no longer fears the wrath of the God of Moses.

No matter! She will forget the callous Judería, which sees no difference between vice and passion...

But how terrible to never see her native country again! To run away without a kiss from her old father who may soon die!

Large tears roll down Mazaltob's cheeks.

In her thoughts, his large crystal-clear blue eyes dim and light up again.

Courage! Cost what it may, tomorrow she will run away.

... But how filled with suffering is her happiness!

Chapter 14

Two a.m.

The Judería, haunted by solitude, has fallen asleep.

Against the silence from afar, a mournful groaning comes from a house that death has called upon tonight.

Street lamps are out, their oil spent. Darkness.

* * *

In the intermittent pallor emanating from a cloudy moon a door is ajar, and a stealthy figure is hiding in the shadows . . .

A man, most likely, because the figure is wrapped in the kind of hooded cloak often donned by rabbis and hahamim.

* * *

But what sort of man walks so gingerly, so fearfully?

Mazaltob—for it is she who walks—presses her hand on her racing heart. A fear of being in the night, alone, a fear of running into someone she knows and of being recognized . . . and a fear, the greatest of all, of the deed she is about to carry out . . .

* * *

Jean is right there, only a hundred meters away, she knows it.

But will she have the courage to reach the street corner where she must meet him? Oh! How hard it is to change your life!

* * *

The moon is now entirely covered. At each step, the ankles of the fugitive twist on the rough stones that stick out from the ground.

Will she ever get there?

Mazaltob

But from a corner, a dark shape breaks away. Two arms tenderly embrace the young woman, while an ecstatic voice whispers: "Darling..."

The Judería, bewildered, beholds an unprecedented spectacle: two intertwined shadows headed toward happiness.

* * *

Ah! This winding Judería whose streets flow like endlessly intersecting canals!

* * *

Mazaltob recalls last night's dream: Like tonight, she was running away, but it was, then, at the quick, muffled speed of a ghost. Like tonight, too, in which one street ceaselessly spawns another street. Deep within the narrow perspective of two extending walls, one could hazard the far vision of a landscape bathed in moonlight...

And then Mazaltob lunged toward the landscape, toward the horizon, toward the freedom... But the narrow streets kept getting longer... and longer... Those streets seemed to whisper to her: "The Judería controls you: you will not break free."

"Darling, we are out of the Jewish quarter."

Indeed, the air smells like freedom.

But they must still walk for a long time before they reach the city's gates, behind which await Charles Balder and the armed escorts who will protect these travelers on the perilous journey from Tetouan to Tangier.

The young Frenchman has bought everyone's silence with *hassanis*— the Moroccan currency, and with Spanish *pesetas.* He has tended to every detail. Mazaltob and Jean will reach the Moroccan city only three hours prior to the departure of the ship to Marseille on which they must sail.

As for Charles Balder, he will remain a few more days in Tetouan to take on the challenging role of appeaser before the Macíases.

* * *

Each tiny house, in the rural area they've now reached, fearfully hides behind a small fence. Orange trees stare at the road beyond garden walls.

Above, in a sky cleansed of its mists, the stars peek out one at a time.

And then Phoebe's golden face reappears, illuminating Tetouan's nearby ramparts . . . Freedom.

*   *   *

They've walked in silence until now, very fast, set on the idea to run away as quickly as possible. Feeling nearly safe in these last moments before their journey on horseback, they would love to relish their solitude for a moment, away from their guides.

*   *   *

It's a night in April, one of those African Aprils rife with powerful scents; one of those nights which, if you've ever lost a lover, leaves you full of regret.

With a trembling hand, Jean lowers Mazaltob's hood and in the moonlight her splendid, dark Madonna face suddenly appears.

That face, so beautiful . . . so beautiful, that Jean cannot resist his desire to bring it close to his.

His mouth lays feverishly on her forehead, redolent of white jasmine, then follows the perfect curve of her eyebrows, and comes to linger on her soft eyelids, so soft they seem like other lips under his lips . . . And here, here is her cheek, smooth as fine porcelain . . . And finally her ear shaped like a shell . . .

*   *   *

A soft breeze rises, injecting headier perfumes in the air.

Jean senses the voluptuous roundness of her breast against his chest . . . Frenzied, aroused, he tightens his embrace and takes Mazaltob's lips in his.

It's a fierce, almost cruel kiss . . . a deep kiss . . . a kiss that violates the barrier of her teeth . . . a kiss that penetrates . . . penetrates and digs . . .

*   *   *

Jean has lost all sense of himself, so much so that he doesn't feel two desperate hands pushing him away. He can't see that body wrestling like a person in agony.

He understands his misfortune only when she, her entire body stiff, succeeds in breaking away . . ."I cannot . . . I cannot . . . Leave without me," she stammers.

Mazaltob

And already she leaps into the night.
She runs... She runs... She is far...

* * *

So far that she can't see a shadow lying still atop the black earth, hands outstretched.

Chapter 15

May 1911.

I write this letter, Mazaltob, with a broken heart, for I know something dreadful, my love: I shall never see you again.

No, I shall never see you again . . . For that cold clinic I once entered lying on a stretcher I shall now leave lying down, though this time it will be inside a coffin.

Never again! All the world's despair is for me enclosed in those words. There was once a time, which now seems so distant, when I, like Werther,[1] on the cusp of youth and of life, would have been moved by the scent of acacias in May, which flowed from every street.

But why would anything matter to me now that you have given me the greatest happiness as well as the greatest sorrow? Mazaltob, you by whom I die, how happy we might have been together! For you too shall suffer, my love: your heart is mine, even though your body belongs to that other man you did not love.

Were roses to open in January, were the sun to rise at midnight, and Tetouan to become a new Sodom, nothing in this world would change this fact: within you lie two conflicting sides that can never be reconciled.

Alas! It is only on the threshold of death that I fathom that truth . . . Too late . . .

Ah, if only I had known . . .

Oh Mazaltob, I fancied you different, very different from that woman of Tetouan you bear inside: For you loved only the books I loved, and your dreams had only the color of my dreams. Among the girls of your country, your forehead was perhaps the only one to feel the burden of the Judería's yoke, for you spoke to me in my father's tongue. And in your voice, I heard, when you sang, the sweetness and passion that by turns haunts my French and my Russian soul.

How foolish I was! On the scale of races, opposite the tray of prejudice and ancestral beliefs, I cast the weight of your aspirations. As if each human being did not, despite herself, heed those myriad injunctions dictated by her ancestry! We think to be ourselves, but we are really those who have come before us.

Had you lived in a place other than your native city, perhaps you might have escaped the atavistic loyalty you shared with the women of your blood. Like so many of your sisters, you needed only to leave Tetouan to become free.

But then I kissed you. I kissed you with a kiss so tender and so savage that it showed that the shape of your body was as dear to me as your thoughts.

If only I had known! . . .

Ah! Forgive me. I was only a man . . . a man, like all other men, weak and violent at once. Nonetheless . . . If only I had known!

My love was perhaps strong enough to find sustenance in itself. I could have been content with your cherished presence.

To live under the radiance of your unforgettable eyes, I would still have been content.

But soon I shall die . . . No, I am already dead. I died in Tetouan that night in April when you abandoned me . . . I died begging Charles Balder, who had rushed to my rescue, not to bring you back to me—what good would it have served?

And then, lying in my friend's arms, my heartbeats ripping my chest apart, I experienced, with difficulty, in painful stages, the nocturnal ride that should have led me to my happiness. At last, the waves' furious plaint echoed louder than my weeping.

And now, my poor sick body quitting once and for all, I perish, as my father did, under the skies of a French town.

I had dreamt of your hand on my forehead at the time of my death. Instead, I'll have a nurse for whom I'll be nothing more than number three, who "has just passed away"!

Mazaltob, I have often told you this: I dread those graves that the Judeo-Christian tradition has devised. As a poet, my dreams are populated with funerary urns garlanded with flowers, as in Ancient Greece. But I wished for something even better. Indeed, I yearned for my ashes to be scattered by a friendly hand on my cherished Pyrenean retreat. Of my remains, each blade of grass will have soaked up a molecule . . .

But you, too, Beloved, will die, and at the thought of resting far from the land in which you shall rest, I grow more despondent. I ask that my body be brought back to Tetouan and—may your God, if He's real, forgive me—that I rest in the Jewish cemetery that one day will take you in.

To be admitted in that cemetery, since I am not Jewish, I bequeath my entire fortune to the needy of Tetouan.

There will be neither Hebrew epitaph nor Latin requiescat on my gravestone, but rather, only these words:

HEREIN LIES JEAN

WHO LOVED AND DIED.

And now, Mazaltob, I shall prepare myself for the harrowing torments of agony... May your name, repeated to my last breath, serve as the saintly Shema of Israel and as the Christian Holy Viaticum.[2]

And since all is permitted to the dying, allow me to give you once again that sweet and terrible kiss, which, alas, drove us apart.

Mazaltob, I kiss you with all my flesh, that same flesh soon to be nullified; Mazaltob, I kiss you with all my soul, which is, perhaps, immortal. Oh, you, who will not close my eyes... Mazaltob, my last thought, Mazaltob, farewell.

* * *

In the Jewish cemetery, next to Jean's grave, there is room for another grave. It is rumored that space has been secretly purchased by a woman.

Doctor Bralakoff has traveled to Tetouan with Jean's remains—Jean, who was a son to him without being one.

What sorrow gave the *coup de grâce* to his heart, forever weakened by a distant pogrom? The poor man would like to know.

In vain he wonders. Jean and Charles Balder disappeared one night, leaving everyone in the Judería astonished. No one is able to say more.

But Serge's father pursued his painful inquiry. An old Jew living by the city's gates, one April night, saw some guides on horseback on the road. There were two foreigners, one fair and terribly pale, looking very ill, held by another, riding double—his friend, no doubt.

The old Jew knows nothing else.

Seeing Mazaltob's face, Doctor Bralakoff understood it all.

* * *

She speaks to no one, but ceaselessly whispers to herself verses he once left between the pages of a book, verses not even meant for her—for she

126

stirred him too much for there to be poetic cadence to his thinking—verses written while in a Pyrenean retreat, a night that Nature, his second beloved, had snatched from his poet's soul.

Mindless of who listened, she repeats those verses. Obsessed with them, she recites them time and again:

> *It is then, in the radiant and somber hour of sunset*
> *When its reflection on the lake inflames branches,*
> *And when to the East the verdant horizon exhales a sleepy sigh.*
> *And the moon etches white horns in the sky.*
> *And a flower appears to catch in its chalice*
> *A shard of daylight which, from the flesh of its petals,*
>   *illuminates it.*
> *That, despite the shimmering lights from the West,*
> *Dusk, like a conspiracy, weaves its nightly web.*

Like a conspiracy, despite the shimmering lights from the West, dusk weaves its nightly web... The same had been true for her, for Mazaltob...

Despite the intellectual light coming from the North, her blood spun the dark conspiracy of instinct within her...

Nothing separated her from Jean... not even her own God... Yet she could not escape the Judería from which her soul had broken free...

Did she regret obeying the instinct of the woman from Tetouan?... She does not know... She no longer knows... Each passing day blurs her thinking even more...

* * *

The doctors have told the family: "Do not upset her... It would kill her..." So, they let her be.

They let her go every day to the cemetery, followed from afar by a man from the Judería to keep the Arabs at bay: She is so beautiful, with her hair, which she forgot to put up, unfastened, and her thin face, in which the circles under her eyes make them appear even larger, nearly unreal!

She goes, indifferent to the cruel gibes from children, indifferent to the summer sun striking her skull, its rays harsher each day.

But at the gates of the necropolis, she turns, her eyes wild, and whoever

127

has followed her there must carefully hide to not see her convulsing on the ground, screaming like a rabid animal.

Insensitive to the torrid heat of July, lithe, she hoists herself amidst the graves. And then she finally stops, kneels down, and lays her lips on a gravestone with a short epitaph for a long, heartbreaking kiss...

One afternoon of scorching African heat, Mazaltob's neck failed to rise...

* * *

She lay in the bedroom of her elder sister.

The entire family has rushed to her side. Hidden behind the bedposts is the head of the Hevra, whose unerring eye predicts the time of her last sigh.

She doesn't move.

Her brothers and sisters are there. So too are old David and Salomon, their white beards moist with tears... And her eyes, which she opens all at once, recognize no one...

But as Preciada noisily bursts into tears, Mazaltob slowly lifts her head: her gaze, descending from that land of indifference in which the dying rest before the final torments, wavers.

Her erstwhile lucidity returns, that dreadful lucidity which often precedes someone's last moments.

She knows the hour of supreme solitude has come... after a life of equal solitude amidst her kin, both so loving and so lacking in understanding...

Jean... her beloved Jean... will she find him again... there?

* * *

All at once a voice cries out:

"Dearest sister... Nothing will remain of your passage on this earth for you have not, as I, known the great joys of motherhood..."

And Mazaltob heard. And Mazaltob answers, from the depths of her frailty:

"Poor Preciada, poor fool who prides herself on spawning eyes that will soon cry, chests that one day will pant under the implacable grip of agony..."

Mazaltob

But the gaze of the moribund girl is already gone, staring past those in attendance at something faraway, something dreadful which makes her shiver.

Silence.

Breathless silence... A fierce game of waiting in which death is dancing with life...

But Mazaltob's body, which has felt only twenty-one summers and winters, is not yet ready to be snatched by the forces of the Unseen.

A song suddenly makes its way from her mouth to her colorless lips.

A song so tenuous, so tenuous that everyone, cocking their heads to listen, can scarcely recognize.

> *"Seven years I have waited.*
> *And seven more I shall wait.*
> *Fourteen years have ended, and if he still has not returned,*
> *A nun I shall become,*
> *A nun like Saint Clare,*
> *A nun like Doña Ines..."*

Her large eyes open again, filled with the tears of the dying.

"Mazaltob," whispers her breathless mouth, "Mazaltob... that name which means good luck..."

* * *

Her words' last syllables fade as the poignant death rattle begins.

The head of the Burial Society signals. The men approach, and the Shema calmly resounds: "Hear, O Israel: Adonaï is our God, Adonaï is One."

* * *

Preciada lets out a piercing scream. She is at once taken away. Nothing must disrupt the fervor of their prayers! Satan is there, lurking in the dark, waiting for a chance to snatch off a departing soul.

The wall of voices grows tighter, and lifts, lifts, higher and higher:

"Hear, O Israel, Adonaï is our God, Adonai is one...Hear, O Israel: Adonaï is our God, Adonaï is One..."

...Two pious hands touch her eyelids, and lay out a sheet, as a first shroud, on her dreadfully white face.

Mazaltob is dead.

THE END

Mazaltob and the Rise of the Modern Sephardi Novel

YAËLLE AZAGURY

Sumptuously dressed in the local "Berberisca" costume, a solemn crown called "sfifa" around her head, rouge on her cheeks and henna on her nails, she keeps her eyes closed all the way so that her husband is the first man she will see upon arrival.

Family and friends have preceded her.

The piyyut "Yaalat Hen" rises to the now mostly darkened sky. The entire neighborhood is watching at their windows and doorsteps.

You...You...You...You...

The flower of all flowers has left her home.

With the "nahora," a huge lantern illuminating its path, the procession courses through the tiny streets of the Judería.

You...You...You...You...

The father bestows on the most prominent men the honor of carefully guiding the blind steps of his daughter.

And Mazaltob, with eyes shut, is led to her destiny.

—*MAZELTOB*

This passage, which describes the wedding ceremony of the Jews of Morocco called Berberisca, exemplifies the intricacies of Bendahan's writing. On the one hand, it is a faithful, even intimate rendering of a marriage tradition to which Moroccan Jews, wherever they reside, are to this day deeply attached. Note, for instance, the sudden irruption of the narrator in the text: the sentence "the flower of all flowers has left her home" betrays her personal involvement in the moment. Note, too, the palpable emotion arising at the sound of the marriage melody, which the theatricality of the account accentuates. The narrator (Bendahan, presumably, though we will see that the narrative voice in *Mazaltob* is slippery) appears to speak from within.

On the other hand, it is simultaneously a description that betokens the narrator's distance from that custom. That narrator presents the ceremony as an objectifying spectacle. We, readers, are watching, just like "the entire neighborhood at their windows and doorsteps." An automaton with no will of her own, Mazaltob is also portrayed externally.

In upholding this dual gaze in her writing, in interweaving contra-dictory narrative voices, Bendahan's originality advanced, in her time, the purpose of a new literary genre.[1] That genre is the modernist Sep-hardi novel, which first appeared at the turn of the century from a male vantage point, under the impulse of Sadia Lévy (also an Algerian Jew) in his novel *Rabbin* (1896), written in French.[2] Focusing on *Mazaltob*, the characteristics of this new genre will be discussed in this essay. They include an allegiance to French culture, a devotion to and an affection for one's own religious and cultural traditions, a multilingualism and cosmopolitanism, and a position both privileged and uncomfortable as cultural intermediary.

An Orientalist Novel by a Jewish Woman?

At first glance, *Mazaltob* might be construed as an Orientalist novel. For throughout the nineteenth century and well into the twentieth, any historian, anthropologist, or philologist who wrote, taught, or conducted research about "the Orient" was considered an Orientalist. As a specialist who probed, elucidated, and explained the culture and traditions of the Sephardi Jews to a French audience, Blanche Bendahan was no doubt, in this sense, a knowledgeable Orientalist.

A second meaning of Orientalism, however, proposed by Edward Said forty years ago in a groundbreaking book titled *Orientalism*, defines it instead as "a style of thought based upon an ontological and episte-mological distinction made between 'the Orient' and 'the Occident.'" According to Said, that distinction facilitated "a Western style for making statements about the Orient," and for "dominating, restructuring, and having authority about it."[3] In short, it created and legitimized a hierarchy between East and West, in which the West controlled the discourse on the East. While the first definition of Orientalism is positive, the second, associated with colonial domination, is not.

These two diametrically opposed definitions—one positive, the other negative—paradoxically converge in Bendahan's work. That it is both an outsider's view which constructs a fallacious binary between the West (France, especially) and the "Orient," and, at the same time, an insider's thorough knowledge of Tetouan, is what makes *Mazaltob* so intriguing for today's readers.

The story opens to a fairy-tale description of Mazaltob, the eponymous heroine of the novel, who is portrayed as beautiful, intelligent, hard-working, and kind. An Oriental atmosphere settles in from the outset, as Mazaltob is seen as an exotic Shulamit, King Solomon's beloved. The conflation of the Jew and the Oriental is a common trope of the time— frequent, for instance, in Proust's *A la recherche du temps perdu*, first published only eleven years earlier. Think for example of Albert Bloch, a Jewish friend of the narrator, who is likened to the Ottoman Sultan Mehmet II in the portrait by the Venetian painter Giovanni Bellini. Or in another description of Bloch yet again who, with his goatee beard and a "glove which he carries like a roll of papyrus in his hand" [...] "com-pletely satisfies a certain taste for the oriental."[4] That trope can also be traced to Pierre Benoît's novel *Le Puits de Jacob* (1925), which tells the story of the Jewish dancer Agar Moses born in Constantinople, and it populates the immensely successful works of the Tharaud brothers, as well as the equally popular novels of the Algerian Jewish writer Elissa Rhaïs. So great was the hunger for exoticism in 1920s France that Rhaïs, whose real name was Rosine Boumendil (she was a Jewish woman from Blida in Algeria), was even presented by her publishing house Plon as a mysterious Muslim woman who had escaped the harems of the Orient and was privy to their alluring secrets.

In many ways, Blanche Bendahan complies with the Orientalist per-spective of the day, immersed as she was in an atmosphere which con-strued Western civilization as superior. In the first chapter, for example, a series of privative clauses define Mazaltob, as though she were a receptacle waiting to be filled: "She has never played in a park... neither has she played in a garden... nor has she played in a farm." Similarly, the narrow and mineral space of the Judería is at once contrasted with the verdant cities of France. This is a recurring binary in contemporaneous novels, which picture the *mellah*, or Jewish quarter, as closed off, circular, and insalubrious, in opposition to the vast and healthy horizons of Europe.[5]

When we first meet her, Mazaltob is a determined student desirous of learning math, despite her brothers' indifference. She is likely to fulfill the promise of happiness contained in her name, which means good fortune. Literally and metaphorically, she possesses her own voice—she takes singing lessons with Madame Gérard, the French consul's wife. But Mazaltob grows voiceless once she is married off to José Jalfon, a Tetouani émigré to Buenos Aires. On her wedding day, she is like a wedding postcard of Orientalist fantasy—an enigma, impenetrable and impassive as the Orient. As in the realist novels of Balzac and Zola, in which characters are reflections of their milieu, Mazaltob gradually becomes an emanation of her environment, slowly ensnared in stone-like Tetouan. Described as a "statue," she is further objectified under José Jalfon's gaze, which reduces her to a block of marble when he realizes that "of her, only her body he will possess." Stripping Mazaltob of her individuality and interiority, José projects onto her the quintessential Orientalist gaze.

That Orientalist perspective is upheld in other familiar ways, too. Its predictable tropes of whiteness and blackness, for example, frequently recur. From nature (clouds, seafoam, jasmine) to the similes Bendahan employs (egg whites, marble, camellias) to Mazaltob's "extraordinarily white face," the continual reappearance of whiteness denotes aesthetic beauty while also conveying the usual moral qualities culturally associated with unmixed, untainted white. In contrast, Mazaltob's immaculately white face is pierced with her "eyes of black diamond," and it is similarly framed by "jet black hair." Furthermore, Mazaltob's whiteness distinguishes her from her dark-skinned sister Preciada. Mazaltob is, physiognomically, an anomaly in this place and time.

The portrayal of a subject as "white" does not, however, signal her as European—rather, just the opposite. As in Orientalist art, the object of desire is always pictured as white. Think of Jean-Dominique Ingres's painting *La Petite Baigneuse*, of his *Turkish Bath*, or of Jean-Léon Gérôme's *Le Bain*, to name only a few.[6] So, too, does Mazaltob's overdetermined whiteness signal her as "exotic." In Bendahan's novel, whiteness designates Mazaltob as at once "enticingly other and reassuringly familiar," an object for Orientalist delight.[7] Her sister Preciada is presented as her foil. Juxtaposing Mazaltob's pallor with Preciada's brownness might be read as "conjoining rather than contrasting" the two sisters—black and white combined in a quintessential Orientalist fantasy.[8]

The binding together in the novel of blackness and whiteness points to another trope ubiquitous in the literature of this era in France: the *Belle Juive*, or the archetypal young Jewish woman. The Belle Juive, or beautiful Jewess, is an avatar of Orientalism, but it also has tropes of its own. Since her first appearance in European literature as Rebecca in Walter Scott's *Ivanhoe*, this figure is filled with ambiguity, her beauty both alluring and disturbing. She is, in effect, an interstitial denizen of both East and West. Being neither entirely dark nor perfectly white, her physical appearance further mirrors that duality. Inquiring about Mazaltob before he meets her, José Jalfon asks: "Is she blonde or brunette?" A question to which one character replies that: "her eyes and her hair are brown, but her skin is that of a blonde." Both black and white, blonde and brunette, sensuous and pure, the Belle Juive is a blank slate of (Christian) fantasies about Jews and Jewishness, sometimes reflecting philosemitism and sometimes antisemitism.[9]

Bendahan rejects the irksome Belle Juive portraits found in the ambiguously antisemitic descriptions of her contemporaries, for example the Frères Tharaud. As one might expect from a Jewish writer, hers instead is a favorable portrait of the Jewish woman. Mazaltob embodies Israel's primeval dignity through her resemblance with "Shulamit," King Solomon's beloved, a Biblical beauty often summoned in portraits of Belles Juives. Her purity is also moral. Not only does Mazaltob remain unsullied by her husband's moral corruption, but she also appears as a sinless, even virginal, figure. Though the text remains discreet as to whether she has engaged in sexual relations (we oddly learn nothing of her wedding night with José Jalfon), she has all the attributes of a maternal figure. She is the caretaker for her baby sister after her own mother dies in childbirth. Sexualized in the gaze of José and Jean, she is not, however, portrayed as a sexual creature herself. Rather, it's the opposite: she shuns sexuality. In the novel, kissing (and hence lust) is problematic. A kiss, as in Sleeping Beauty, brings Jean back to life in one instance, but in another has dire consequences.

Mazaltob, though Jewish, is encoded as a Marian figure. She has no children with José, whose name significantly derives from the name Joseph. The portrayal of a Jewish woman as a Christian figure is, however, paradoxical.[10] How to account for it? The Belle Juive is more readily viewed in a favorable light because Jewish women, who wept at the crucifixion of Jesus, showed compassion for his suffering. They are markedly more susceptible to conversion to Christianity than Jewish men, who are doomed to be cursed. While Jewish men are viewed as capable of deicide, Jewish women are construed as matricial figures. Symbolizing the continuity between the Old and the New Testament, these women thus emerge as a link between Judaism and Christianity. Judaism is hence reinterpreted as a matrix to Christianity. That image is entirely pertinent to Bendahan's presentation of Judaism in the novel. It derives from the captivating turn intellectual debates took in France at the time.

France in the 1920s: An Experimental Laboratory for Ideas about Jewishness

Though often amalgamated with the darkly antisemitic 1930s, the 1920s in France merit separate scrutiny. This may come as a surprise. The Dreyfus Affair, revealing deep strands of antisemitism in nineteenth-century France, had profoundly scarred French society in the last years of the century, jeopardizing the hard-won integration of its Jews. But after the First World War, victory encouraged a new sense of optimism and a renewed trust in the equality of all men. Immigration laws of the '20s were laxer and more welcoming. In generating opportunities for social mixing and fraternizing, the war had further promoted the identification of Jews with the French Nation and advanced their incorporation into French society. Checked by left-leaning governments of the 1920s, antisemitic sentiment in France, unlike in Germany, receded. Zionism, giving Judaism a new sense of direction, energized both directly and indirectly debates on Jewish selfhood. Fresh hopes for a Jewish future, as well as a renewed self-reflectiveness, blossomed among Jews.

The success of Marcel Proust's *A la recherche du temps perdu* is emblematic of the times. The second volume, *A L'ombre des jeunes filles en fleurs (Within a Budding Grove)*, which appeared in 1919, marks the beginning of the period in which this shift occurs. Though many decried Proust's "Jewish sentences," with its endless clauses so antithetical to "classic" French style, his novel won the coveted Prix Goncourt in 1919. Ambivalence toward Jews endured in France in the early years of the new century. Attitudes oscillated between the desire to incorporate Jews into French society by erasing their particularity, and an endemic antisemitism of which anti-Dreyfusard sentiment was symptomatic. Proust was himself half-Jewish, and *La Recherche*, which is a complex plumbing of identity in general, and a reckoning with Jewish identity in particular, reflects his own equivocation. Though he was an ardent Dreyfusard, he was also, in his novel, a vector of the same stereotypes used by the antisemites he opposed. Nonetheless, Jewish characters, who had figured in French literary works since the nineteenth century primarily as bankers, money-lenders, or prostitutes, were now for the first time portrayed with greater complexity. Charles Swann, the principal character of *La Recherche* and a Jew, attests to this change.

In choosing the theme of identity as one of the kernels of his novel, Proust laid the first stone in the edifice to demystify the clichés of the past. The 1920s teemed with new and often positive ideas about Judaism and Jewishness—an effervescence which has caused several historians to speak of a "réveil Juif" (Jewish awakening), evident in the birth of Jewish magazines such as *Menorah* (1922) or *La Revue Juive* (1925).[11] No longer narrowly focused on Jewish communal matters, the concerns of these new periodicals became instead literary and cultural. Novels, short stories, and essays, predominantly by Jewish authors, flowered, riding the vogue of regionalist, folkloric, and exotic literature. In 1926, the Prix Renaudot was awarded to Armand Lunel, a Provençal Jew. Soon thereafter, in 1931, *Mazaltob* won a Prix de l'Académie Française, of which no more than sixty are awarded each year. This recognition unofficially capped the preceding decade and its bountiful philosemitic production.

During that decade, the non-Jewish Parisian world timidly began to pay attention to this proliferation. Choosing to write in his column on "French literature" for *les Nouvelles Littéraires* rather than for a Jewish publication, Jewish critic Benjamin Crémieux penned in 1925 an essay titled "Judaïsme et Littérature" in which he took stock of this new phenomenon.[12] In France, he observed, Jewishness was in fashion.

This new consciousness, which came from Jews and non-Jews alike, was not without ambivalence, and ran the gamut from overt philosemitism to a masked antisemitism best embodied by the Frères Tharaud, whose stories were surprisingly well-received in Jewish circles. Jewishness was henceforth an open and uninhibited topic for discussion. Any interest was construed as laudable curiosity.

Consider, for instance, the frequent use in literature of the era of expressions such as "l'âme juive," "la race juive," "l'atavisme juif," etc.[13] *Mazaltob* is filled with such examples. "Atavism," a murky term, circulated undisturbed in the fin-de-siècle. Though used primarily in the racist theories which flowered in the nineteenth century, it also recurred in the progressive science of the time, and in the medical theories of physiognomy, now widely discredited, which had been developed by the Italian doctor Cesare Lombroso, a phrenologist, criminologist, and also a Jew. Other prominent Jewish thinkers of the time, such as Max Nordau (1848–1923), endorsed them as well.[12] After liberating themselves from life in the narrow and airless streets of the ghetto in the preceding centuries of oppression, "regeneration," Nordau believed, would ensue, and a new Jewish man would be born.

Regeneration—and especially Jewish regeneration—was a key concept of that era. It permeated the ideas of the Wissenchaft des Judentum (i.e., modern critical historico-philological Jewish studies), a German-Jewish movement that sought to emancipate the practice of Judaism from centuries of "moral corruption," and to create a secular science of Judaism.[14] It also prevailed in the rhetoric of the Alliance Israélite Universelle as well as in *Mazaltob*, where the stifling and gossipy atmosphere of the frozen Judería is contrasted with the enlarged vistas Mazaltob experiences by the shore in Kitane.

Other Jewish debates with which *Mazaltob* engages appear as well. Jean's Christian friend Charles Balder, who is present in the novel's second half, voices the views of Catholic Revivalism, an underexplored ecumenical movement. This philosemitic current emerged in Paris in the early years of the twentieth century, in the wake of the Dreyfus affair's toxic antisemitism. Figures such as the writer Charles Péguy (1873–1914), Léon Bloy (1846–1917), and Raïssa Maritain (1883–1960) were engaged in a recasting of the relationship between Judaism and Christianity.[15] They sought an alternative both to traditional Christian contempt of Judaism and to the Republic's *laïcité* with its avowed secularism and dismissal of particularity.

Catholics were encouraged to regard Judaism as a probe with which to scrutinize their own spirituality (or lack thereof). Similarities between the two faiths were emphasized, and hence friendship between the two "sister" religions highlighted. Péguy eloquently expressed his quest for harmony between Jews and Christians in the following lines: "So similar, so different; such enemies, such friends; such strangers, so much penetrated by one another, so intertwined; so allied and so loyal; so opposite and so conjoined."[16]

Bendahan echoes this sentiment throughout Mazaltob. In highlighting Jewish hardship as a dignifying ordeal, Bendahan also hints at another theme favored by Péguy—namely, the Jew as the ideal sufferer. According to Péguy, affliction—Léon Bloy would go one step further in using the more vexing notion of "abjection"—elevates the Jew to a state of holiness that Christians must emulate.

The Revivalist movement was not exempt from stereotypes and essentializing characterizations about Jews, of the sort one also encounters in *Mazaltob*. Furthermore, while Péguy cared little for the conversion of Jews to Christianity, Léon Bloy, who believed that Christianity was the future of Judaism, was less circumspect. The spiritual journey of poet and philosopher Raïssa Maritain (née Oumançoff), a student of Péguy and then of Léon Bloy, amplified and extended Bloy's spiritual pursuits. Maritain was born in Russia to a Jewish family that had fled the pogroms to settle in Paris. Under Léon Bloy's guidance, she later converted to Christianity, though she did not see her Jewishness as suppressed by her Christianity.[17] Impelled by her pursuit of Christian-Jewish unity, she and her husband Jacques held a salon at Meudon, outside Paris, from 1923 to 1939. Jews and non-Jews alike flocked to these gatherings, attracted by the novelty of the explorations the salon conducted and the fluidity it sought between the two faiths. Was Blanche Bendahan apprised of these far-reaching spiritual pursuits in the Métropole? Undoubtedly so. She had spent crucial years of her childhood and her adolescence in France, and her mother was Catholic, as was her stepmother, Marie Ginoux. Blanche thus walked a thin line between Judaism and Christianity. Or perhaps, as with other

French Jews, she was actively searching for an assimilationist paradigm which would sustain at once her North African Jewishness and her Frenchness. Nevertheless, *Mazaltob* is, as its dedication earnestly stipulates, "a Jewish novel." Even when humorous or satirical, its descriptions of the quaintness of the customs of Jewish Tetouan never cease to be tender. But, as in all other matters, the novel's stance on religion is elusive—its spiritual quest stretching beyond Judaism. Jean, for instance, believes in a "cosmic God who juggles both nebulae and sun"—a stance that brings him close to theism. José, his cruder nemesis, is equally free-spirited, but his cynicism prevents him from holding on to any faith or belief. Doctor Bralakoff cares not for a "literalist" practice of Judaism, but instead for the respect of its spirit. And Uncle Salomon pleads for a conservative but pragmatic observance informed by a set of ethical principles. By the novel's end, *Mazaltob*, albeit a Jewish novel, also hints at a path beyond the Jewishness for which it so fervently pleads.

Jewishness and Beyond: *Mazaltob*'s Hybridization and Its Experimentation with Novel Literary Forms

Just as Bendahan searched for a commodious religious structure in which Jewishness and Christianity might harmoniously coexist, so, too, does her writing explore a hybrid literary space, in which she experiments with multiple linguistic and literary traditions.

There has been in recent years much talk in postcolonial literary theory on hybridity and hybridization (the process by which hybridity is obtained). Coined in the first half of the twentieth century by literary critic Mikhaïl Bakhtine, the term was defined as "a mixture of two social languages within the limits of a single utterance, as an encounter, within the arena of an utterance, between two different linguistic consciousnesses, separated from one another by an epoch, by social differentiation or by some other factor."[18] Contemporary commentators have appropriated the concept to apply it to recent novelistic developments by postcolonial writers. Praising the cross-pollination fostered by hybridization, also called *métissage*, these critics have observed that several postcolonial writers in the late twentieth and early twenty-first century successfully blended the multiple threads that composed their history and their identity, thus breathing new life into old novelistic forms. Salman Rushdie and V. S. Naipaul are often cited as prime examples of this trend. The notion of hybridity, however, has never been used in reference to Sephardi literature during or after colonization, for which it appears to be ideally suited.

In weaving together various languages—Haketía, French, and Spanish—mixing high and low registers, blending seemingly disparate cultural references (the Sephardic ballad "Escuchís, señor soldado" with Baudelaire or Lamartine), and finally, fashioning, through the use of internal focalization—a technique by which the narrator's voice is coextensive with the voice of a chosen character—a slippery narrative voice which defeats a single authoritative discourse, *Mazaltob* offers a remarkable illustration of the polyphony achieved through hybridization.

Speaking of Preciada's sallow complexion, the narrator reports:

> "Marriage will cure that," the elderly ladies say.
> In the slightest cold weather, her already thick fingers swell with blisters.
> Marriage will also cure that.
> Preciada is grumpy because of her stomach ailments.
> Marriage will cure both her stomach and her grumpiness.

Whose voice is that? It appears to be spoken by a diffuse public opinion—a voice akin to the chorus in Greek tragedy ("the elderly ladies"). But who speaks in a sentence like the following: "marriage will cure both her stomach and her grumpiness"? Is it the aforementioned "elderly ladies," or is it the narrator? And is the statement to be taken at face value? The answer is no. By appropriating the sentence of the "elderly ladies," the seemingly discreet and unassuming narrator uses irony both to mock and subvert their statement.

Bendahan's literary experimentations extend further. Frequently cursory and lacking in detailed descriptions, her style at first glance might be mistaken for hastiness or cliché. But it is rather a carefully constructed combination of diverse social languages and literary modes. Her writing is a blend of high and low in which the naïve and the poetic mingle, and in which formal and informal language intertwine. Oral expressiveness is achieved through frequent anaphoric repetitions. These repetitions frame autonomous vignettes, which are executed in broad brushstrokes on a thought, a situation, or a character. Descriptions are brief, vivacious, sketch-like.

The effect, in the service of Bendahan's satirical tone, is often humorous. Her humor feeds off many sources; folklore is one of them. Consider in the novel, for instance, amusing tales such as "the closed mem," or the story of Friday, Saturday, and Sunday—all of them in the vein of a North African tradition of storytelling, which especially inspired the folktale stories of Djoha, a picaresque and earthy character.

Bendahan combines that source of inspiration with others acquired in her French schooling. There is a dark, moralistic thread in her social satire, evocative of the French tradition of seventeenth-century moralists. As literary critic Paul Reboux wrote, Bendahan is "not only brilliant in her descriptions as well as a caricaturist, but also has the mind of a philosopher."[19] That vein is chiefly evident in her later poems, in a collection titled *Poèmes en short* (1948), for which Bendahan received a Grand Prix de l'Humour, a prestigious French literary prize. The epigraph of *Poèmes en short*, a quote from French eighteenth-century playwright Beaumarchais, is revelatory:

I hasten to laugh of everything, lest I weep of all.

Though it was published much earlier than *Poèmes en short* (1948), *Mazaltob* also counts several occurrences of such humor. Take, for instance, the darkly witty epitaph on Mrs. Macías's grave, in which the myriad household chores Mrs. Macías performed in her lifetime are minutely recorded—a bleak and ironic tribute to the deceased woman.

Bendahan frequently imparts her wisdom with a light touch. *Mazaltob* is a tale with a morality, by turns tenderly chastising and soberly misanthropic, in which the Oranese writer anticipates the deeper philosophizing of the *Poèmes*. There, Bendahan would unmask in light verse the foibles and follies of the human condition. But her vision, though dark, is never despairing. Even pettiness finds grace in her eyes, so long as she can poke fun at it.

A domestic drama, *Mazaltob* also juggles larger themes. "As elsewhere," says its narrator, "in Tetouan, one need only die to be regarded as virtuous." Maxims such as this one pop up frequently—unexpected pearls of wisdom that speak to our shared humanity.

Thematically too, hybridity is the rule. The theme of trespass, for example, is declined in various guises with borrowings from different sources. Bendahan seamlessly interlaces them. For example, *Mazaltob* is a retelling of the story of Sol Hachuel, a traditional tale of Jewish Moroccan folklore, culled from a famous incident which took place in Fez in 1832.[20] That Sol is mentioned in *Mazaltob* is evidence that Bendahan was familiar with the story.

Sol was a beautiful young Jewish girl who lived in Tangier with her stepmother. In one account, she fell in love with her Muslim neighbor and presumably converted to Islam, but later recanted her conversion. Apprised of her recanting, the Pasha imprisoned her in Fez and urged her to reconsider it, for renouncing Islam was a punishable offense. Nevertheless, Sol refused. In her own words, *Hebrea naci, y Hebrea quiero morir* (I was born a Jew, and I shall die a Jew). In another version, the Pasha falls in love with her and requests that she convert, only to meet her scorn, too. The true story of Sol crystallized in the collective imagination of Moroccan Jews as a cautionary tale against crossing religious boundaries. The story *Sarita Benzaquen* by Elisa Chimenti is a reprise of the story of Sol, to which the tale of Mazaltob is also remarkably faithful.[21] Sarita Benzaquen is a beautiful Jewish girl who falls in love with the dashing Si Mohammed El Marrakchi, who is Muslim. On the night of her escape from home to join him, she turns one more time to kiss the mezuzah, a customary gesture performed by Jews. An elderly man instantly materializes in front of her and leads her to the cemetery, whereupon Sarita realizes that he has taken her to her parents' grave. Understanding that if she leaves with Si Mohammed, her parents would die of grief, she forgoes her plan to elope with Si Mohammed and returns to her parents' home.

Tellingly, Mazaltob is reading *Graziella* by Alphonse de Lamartine, a classic tale of the French Romantic imagination. Though that novel takes place not in Tetouan, but in the Italian island of Procida, its themes are similar to those in *Mazaltob*.[22] The narrator falls in love with Graziella, the daughter of a fisherman who saves him and his companion from shipwreck. After spending time living in their home far from his native Paris, he nurtures the fantasy of taking her back to France with him. One

day, trying to please him, she dresses up in the fancy garb of French aris-
tocratic ladies. Upon seeing her, the narrator, who ought to be enchanted
at this sight, is instead appalled. He realizes that in trying to emulate his
culture, Graziella has crossed a boundary, for she will never be part of his
world. He falls out of love and leaves her. Heartbroken, she dies soon after.
The morality of the tale is similar to that of *Mazaltob*: trespassing will
bring trouble. Not that trespassing was anything Bendahan feared. As a
Jew, a writer, and a woman, the crossing of boundaries was familiar to her.

Bendahan's spirited feminism—an essential theme running through
Poèmes en short—is a key motif in *Mazaltob* as well, one which functions
as a vigorous counterpoint to the novel's conventional clichés of Belle
Juives. Reflections on women's enslavement in the household—viewed
as a monstrous Minotaur—abound. Motherhood, either graceless (in
the case of Preciada), lethal (in the case of Mrs. Macías), or unrealized
(in Mazaltob's case), is unwanted or viewed with wariness. Mazaltob will
indeed remain childless, her views on maternity irredeemably hopeless.
In place of the tyrannies of childbearing and the limitations imposed
by consanguinity, Bendahan favors in the novel surrogate parenting and
elective affinities—the adoptive relationship Mazaltob has with Madame
Gérard, a surrogate for her biological mother; the spiritual bond of Doctor
Bralakoff and his nephew Jean; the maternal bond that ties the Jewish
heroine to her youngest sibling, once their mother dies.

While Bendahan pointedly exposed the misogyny among Tetouani
Jews, she viewed the subjugation of women not merely as a Tetouani
phenomenon, but rather as a universal predicament. Just as *Mazaltob* is
an ethnographic narrative scrupulously attentive to geography, so, too, is
it a fable of female enslavement and liberation. For it is about finding
one's true voice, shattering the molds that hold us captive, and breaking
out of our own imaginary prisons. "The gangue of marble still enshrouds
you," says Charles Balder to Mazaltob, whom he likens to a statue being
chiseled out of a block of marble. He adds: "Have courage, please. Keep
fashioning yourself." In so doing, Balder speaks to the fears, desires, and
dilemmas, not only of the woman from Tetouan, but of all women.

Tetouan, then, is as much a condition as it is a place. Sparingly
described, the North African town is one point of a triangle in a symbolic
geography. Tetouan is an imaginary space of confinement, stone-like and

circular. The Jewish cemetery, a place of death, is its quintessential expression. Fundamentally, Mazaltob is a tragic figure. Confined in Tetouan, she cannot find sanctuary in other points of that geography, not in the France of intellectual dialogue, nor in the Spain/Sepharad of romantic longing. Metaphorically, she is always in exile. Though she gradually frees herself from the constraints of tradition, she continually rebuilds imaginary prisons in her mind. Unable to move forward or backward, the young woman, often described as a "statue," remains unsettled, even paralyzed.

The dividedness in which Mazaltob is fatally caught is perhaps one which Blanche Bendahan, despite obvious differences with her character, profoundly understood. The opening poem of Bendahan's *Poèmes en short*, revealingly titled "Janus," gives us a hint. Brimming with antitheses, it seeks to present the poet as a two-faced creature, looking in opposite directions. Her poetry, she writes, melds these oppositions, blends high and low registers.

Though Bendahan stylistically resolved her incongruities in her buoyant yet somber poems, that blending remains elusive in *Mazaltob*. Here, tradition and emancipation persist in an impossible tension. In the novel, Bendahan minutely captures something achingly unresolved. This is inherently new and original for her time. The literary representation of the path to modernity has always been gendered, but most literature traces a young man's path to an autonomous modern life. Seldom does it recount a young woman's journey through the same terrain.

Perhaps Bendahan intimately grasped the audacity of Mazaltob's risk-taking. Perhaps, too, Bendahan's disappearance from our cultural memory stems from the arduousness of her uneasy voice, one which did not fit ready classifications. The writer Bendahan is also an exilic figure. For all that she cared about tradition, she also shunned it. Though her mother was Christian, she embraced her Jewish identity. She lectured on the richness of Sephardi customs, but they did not define her daily life. She spoke fondly of Tetouan, from which her father's family had come, but she also exposed its parochialism. She dreamt of France, but as an adult, only after she had to leave behind her beloved Algeria. By then, her exile had become real.

In *Mazaltob*, Bendahan courageously captures that evanescent instant of fertile in-betweenness, the point at which all possibilities, though still unformed, perhaps even unsaid, are within reach. The novel holds onto the precarious position at which we catch our breath hoping for that promise to become real, lest it vanish forever. Bendahan retraces Mazaltob's perilous journey, one which, as for Orpheus, required her to walk onward, never looking back. Such is the originality of *Mazaltob* that it attempts all of this at once, from the vantage points of both an old and new world. Some may read it as a cautionary tale about the dangers of trespassing. Others will view it as a paean to individual freedom. Shunning illusions of purity, its truths dwell instead on the edges.

The time is ripe to recognize Bendahan as a pioneer of a modern Sephardi feminist literature, one whose relevance continues to resonate in the present, and whose core themes endure in the writing of other Sephardi women writers, among them Jacqueline Kahanoff, Hélène Cixous, Annie Cohen, Paula Jacques, and Chochana Boukhobza.

Acknowledgments

We first "met" in February 2020, thanks to connections made by Matilda Bruckner and Ronnie Scharfman. Frances had discovered *Mazaltob* more than a decade earlier when in Paris and had decided it was time to return to it. Yaëlle had begun a study of four North African Jewish woman writers, which included the author of *Mazaltob*. By the time covid arrived just a month later, the collaboration on an English edition of *Mazaltob* had begun.

We are grateful to so many of our friends and colleagues who came to our assistance and offered their support: Joyce Antler, Olga Borovaya, Saddek Benkada, Gil Chalamish, Linda Clark, Jonathan Decter, Guy Dugas, Alma Heckman, Yuval Evri, Jean-Claude Kuperminc, Jonathan Malino, Susan G. Miller, Megan Marshall, Sergio Parussa, Jason Guberman-Pfeffer, Susan Quinn, Richard Rabinowitz, Jeffrey Specter, Judith Tick, Sonia Cohen Toledano, and Roberta Wollons.

We also thank the skilled and accommodating staff of Brandeis University Press. Working with Sylvia Fuks Fried, Sum Ramin along with Ann Brash, Ashley Burns and Ally Findley has been for both of us a delight.

Notes

Introduction

1. Blanche Bendahan, "Visages de Tétouan," *Les Cahiers de L'Alliance Israélite Universelle (Paix et Droit)*, no. 093 (November 1955): 5.

2. Blanche Bendahan, *Mazaltob*. (Paris: Éditions du Tambourin, 1930).

3. Blanche Bendahan, "Les Sephardim et le romancero Judéo-Castillan," *Les Cahiers de l'Alliance Israélite Universelle (Paix et Droit)*, no. 107 (March 1, 1957): 4–11. This appeared a month before the radio broadcast on April 15, 1957 and without the accompanying music.

4. 1903 often appears as Bendahan's birth date. See for example, the entry for Blanche Bendahan in the *Encyclopedia of Jews in the Islamic World*, ed. Norman Stillman (Leiden: Brill, 2010). The most accurate information, including birth certificates, comes from a family tree compiled by her descendant Pierre Benoliel on Geneanet. https://gw.geneanet.org/pierre benoliel?lang=en&iz=845&p=blanche+jeanne&n=benoliel.

5. Joshua Schreier, *Arabs of the Jewish Faith* (Rutgers University Press, 2010), 25.

6. Saddek Benkada, "A Moment in Sephardi History: The Reestablishment of the Jewish Community of Oran, 1792–1831," in *Jewish Culture and Society in North Africa*, ed. Emily Benichou Gottreich and Daniel J. Schroeter (Indiana University Press, 2011), 175.

7. Marie Ginoux, eight years older than Hayo, has been presumed by scholars to have been Bendahan's teacher rather than her stepmother. See for example Saddek Benkada, "Blanche Bendahan (1893–1975), être écrivain, femme et juive à Oran dans l'entre-deux-guerres (1919–1939)," Société d'Histoire des Juifs de Tunisie, Colloque "Les Juifs du Maghreb de l'époque colonial à nos jours—histoire, mémoire et écritures du passé," Paris, Sorbonne du 3 au 6 novembre 2008, 6.

8. Hayo would marry again in 1908.

9. Cited in Abraham Elmaleh, "Ha-soferet Ha-meshoreret Blanche Bendahan Veyetziroteha Hasifrutiot," *Les cahiers de L'Alliance Israélite* Universelle 4–6, 10e année (mai 1961), 93–96.

10. *Le Droit Des Femmes*, August-September, 1933, 216. Blanche was also a member of the *Comité départemental d'initiative pour l'amnistie aux détenus politiques musulmans*.

11. *Le Droit Des Femmes* (March-April, 1934): 72.

12. *Le Droit Des Femmes* (April, 1936): 60.

13. Saddek Benkada, "Blanche Bendahan," 1.

14. Blanche Bendahan, *Sous les soleils qui ne brilleront plus*, (L'Amitié Par Le Livre, November 25, 1970).

Notes

15. Ibid, 92–3.

16. Ibid, 157–8.

17. Bendahan, "Visages de Tétouan," 7.

18. Abraham Elmaleh, "Ha-soferet Ha-meshoreret . . ."

19. *La Renaissance Politique, Littéraire et Artistique*, 25 October 1930.

20. See Susan G. Miller's compelling analysis of *Mazaltob*. Susan G. Miller, "Gender and the Poetics of Emancipation: The Alliance Israélite Universelle in Northern Morocco, 1890–1912," in *Franco-Arab Encounters*, eds. L. Carl Brown and Matthew S. Gordon (Beirut: American University of Beirut Press, 1996), 229–252.

21. For example, we are told that if the Mosaïc religion, born more than 5,000 years ago, had not vanished from the face of the earth, it was likely due "not to its male but to its female devotees" in Ch. 9 of *Mazaltob*.

22. The announcement for the second edition of *Mazaltob* referred to it as "un classique du Séphardisme." *Les Cahiers de L'Alliance Israélite Universelle (Paix et Droit)*, no.119 (July 1, 1958).

23. In most of Morocco, the Jewish quarter is called the *mellah* ("salt" in Arabic)—so named, it is said, because Jews were obligated to salt the head of anyone who had been executed before sending it to the Sultan, but in fact derived, no doubt, from the salt marsh area of the first *mellah* created in Fez in 1438.

24. Archives of the AIU, Maroc XXXVI.E.625a.

25. Archives of the AIU, Maroc VI. B.25–27.

26. See Susan G. Miller, "Kippur on the Amazon Jewish Emigration from Northern Morocco in the Late Nineteenth Century" in *Sephardi and Middle Eastern Jewries*, ed. H. S. Goldberg (Indiana University Press, 1996), 190–209.

27. Archives of the AIU, Maroc VI.B.25.

28. Archives of the AIU, Maroc LXIV.E.980, June 17, 1896.

29. Shalom Aleichem's famous tale "The Man from Buenos Aires," in which a corrupt Eastern European Jewish man who had emigrated to Argentina returns home in search of a bride, along with recruits for his career as a pimp, comes to mind. See Shalom Aleichem, *Tevye the Dairyman and The Railroad Stories*, trans. Hillel Halkin (New York: Schocken Books, 1987).

30. Archives of the AIU, Maroc LXIV.E 980, July 5, 1894.

31. Archives of the AIU, Maroc LXIV. E. 980, April 20, 1893.

32. Bendahan, *Mazaltob*, Ch.11.

33. Hassiba Coriat, "La femme à toutes les époques de l'histoire," Archives of the AIU, VI. B. 25.

34. Interview by the author with Mesdames F. S. and S. H. in Paris on July 9, 2002.

35. Saddek Benkada, "Blanche Bendahan," 10.

36. Albert Camus, *Lyrical and Critical Essays*, ed. Philip Thody, trans. Ellen Conroy Kennedy (New York: Random House, 1970), 128.

37. Bendahan, *Mazaltob*, Ch. 11.

Notes

38. C. P. Cavafy, "The God Forsakes Antony" in *The Complete Poems of Cavafy*, trans. Rae Dalvin (New York: Harcourt, Brace & World, 1961), 30.

39. Bendahan, *Mazaltob*, Ch. 8.

Mazaltob, Chapter 1

1. [The Judeo-Spanish vernacular of the Sephardim from the North of Morocco is *haketía*. In the Levant, the vernacular is called *ladino* or *judezmo*. Ladino is the literary language of Sephardim, used in prayer books. It is a word-to-word translation of Hebrew. In the Levant, both the literary language and the vernacular Judeo-Spanish are called *ladino*, however. Bendahan provides an incomplete explanation of this linguistic intricacy in Chapter 7.]

2. [Meatballs are a staple of Jewish cooking throughout the Mediterranean.]

3. [*La cabesa* in haketía.]

4. [Judeo-Spanish uses the "b" rather than the "v" sound.]

5. [Jacob Israel Garzón argues that the Tetouani Judería—the Jewish quarter—was the continuation, within a Muslim environment, of the Andalusian *aljamas* from medieval Spain. The aljamas were, rather than ghettos per se, autonomous spaces of Jewish and Muslim self-rule. Although Bendahan places an accent aigu on the "e" of Judería in the French manner, we have opted for the original spelling of the word in Spanish, with the Spanish tilde on the last diphthong.]

6. [Bendahan uses the French spelling (Massias) of this common Sephardi last name. We have chosen instead the Castilian spelling (Macías) favored by the Jews of Tetouan.]

7. [Sephardim means "Spaniards" in Hebrew. It is used for Jews of Iberian origin or those who follow the Iberian rite.]

8. [A "wise man" or "sage" in Hebrew.]

9. [Two important nineteenth-century Rabbis from Tetouan.]

10. ["Cemetery" in haketía. Tetouan's Jewish cemetery is known for its size and antiquity.]

11. [The expression in Spanish is *Cedacito de seda nueva*.]

12. ["Trousseau" in haketía. It is pronounced "ashuar."]

13. A lamentation which means "alas."

14. [*Znoga* means "synagogue" in haketía. By extension, the location for rabbinical studies.]

Mazaltob, Chapter 2

1. [*Bargouelas* are ululations—rhythmical and high-pitched sounds of joy with a trilling quality, which also appear in Arab culture. The joyous you-you sound is the opposite of the somber wo, wo.]

2. [In the original Judeo-Spanish, the ballad is known as "Escuchís, señor soldado":

Escuchís, señor soldado
Si de las guerras venís.
Si señora, de las guerras,
de las guerras del inglès.

Notes

Si habéis visto a mi marido
por fortuna alguna ves.
No conesco a su marido,
ni tampoco sé quien es.

A complete version of this song can be found in Spanish: Arcadio de Larrea Palacín, *Cancionero Judío del Norte de Marruecos. Romances de Tetuán I* (Madrid: CSIC, Instituto de Estudios Africanos, 1952). We have used the translation to haketía by Jacobo Israel Garzón in his Spanish edition of *Mazaltob* (Madrid: Hebraica Ediciones, 2012).]

3. ["European" in Judeo-Spanish.]
4. [*Adafina* is a one-pot meal enjoyed by Sephardim on the Sabbath. It is made with potatoes, sweet potatoes, eggs, chickpeas, and meat. Adafina is considered a predecessor of the Spanish *olla podrida* and of *cocido*.]
5. This refers to a custom in well-to-do Jewish families to knead dough every Thursday night. Bread is then baked on Friday and distributed to the needy on Saturday.
6. A charitable donation for the destitute.
7. *Malograda* means "evildoer" in haketía.
8. [Plural of the Hebrew "ebed."]
9. A good deed done from religious duty.

Mazaltob, Chapter 3

1. [The Wicked Fairy in *Sleeping Beauty*.]
2. [*Con siete manos*, in haketía: an expression which means "willingly" or "eagerly."]
3. Sephardi Jews swear on the life of others to prove that it is dearer than their own.
4. "Those in hand-me-downs aren't used to wearing new pants."
5. [A young Jewish woman from Tangier who was executed in 1834 for refusing conversion to Islam. See the essay at the end of this volume: "*Mazaltob* and the Rise of the Modern Sephardi Novel."]
6. [*Que asi se quede papa*: The expression in haketía is more colorful. It means: "may father remain as he is, that is, alive and well."]
7. ["It is the luck of the plain-looking one that a beauty wishes."]
8. Sister, or *hermana*, is used in Judeo-Spanish as a mark of respect.
9. [This refers to the title of a book by Spanish Senator Angel Pulido. *Españoles sin Patria y la Raza Sefardí* (1905) was the result of an investigation conducted by Pulido among the Sephardi communities of North Africa, the Balkans, and the Ottoman Empire. In his philosemitic campaign Pulido sought full Spanish citizenship for Sephardi Jews.]
10. From *Los Hebreos en Marruecos* by Manuel L. Ortega (p. 267), I translate the following: "The patriotic efforts of our deserving (Spanish) teachers cannot vanquish French influence. Trained to admire the great Trans Pyrenean nation early on, Jews learn and educate themselves only in French... The schools of the Alliance train a cohort of commercial and political agents whose soul is French."

Notes

11. From *Los Hebreos en Marruecos* by Manuel L. Ortega (p. 272), I translate the following: "Mr. Anatole Leroy-Beaulieu says in *the Revue des Deux Mondes* that the Alliance Israélite Universelle in Eastern Europe, in Asia, in Africa, and all around the Mediterranean Sea renders a service to France, one for which French patriotism should be grateful, and which only a sectarian mind would care to ignore...

   "...I should advise that the Jews understand as much as possible the need to "Hispanicize" their education by pledging not to favor the acquisition of a foreign language such as French." *Words spoken by Señor Rivera, delegate of Spain's Central University.*

   "The influence the French have on the Jews of Morocco is noticeable in school and in business." (Ibid, 343)

Mazaltob, Chapter 4

1. [According to Jewish Law, Mazaltob would not have been permitted to sing after marrying.]
2. [The expression in haketía is *escapada de mal*.]
3. A common expression among Sephardim, which holds circumstances alone responsible for someone's absence rather than that person's will.
4. [The Jewish communities of Morocco continue to this day to abide by the laws and rulings of the Takkanot of Castile.]

Mazaltob, Chapter 5

1. [The *lévite* is a long, straight frock coat, somewhat like that worn by a priest.]

Mazaltob, Chapter 6

1. Nine days preceding the Ninth of Av, or Tish'a Be Av, during which meat isn't consumed, except on Saturday.
2. "Move over, sir."

Mazaltob, Chapter 7

1. "Mourners" in Hebrew.
2. Prayer for the dead requiring a quorum of ten men.
3. [Bendahan ignores the long association of the Jews of Spain with the Arabic language.]

Mazaltob, Chapter 8

1. The currency is the Spanish *peseta*. The five- and ten-centimos coins earned the nicknames *perra chica y perra gorda* on account of the lion on the coin, which looked more like a dog.
2. *Nessekh* is the same as *Terefa*—not Kosher—in Hebrew.

Mazaltob, Chapter 9

1. [Hebrew name for Egypt.]
2. [It is actually Exodus 3:3.]

Notes

3. [Haketía.]
4. [Literally "those from underneath" (i.e., the spirits of the Underworld).]
5. [Note that Bendahan provides both the French and Spanish words for sweets.]
6. [The name Sol means "sun" in Spanish.]
7. [The burial society in Jewish tradition.]

Mazaltob, Chapter 10

1. [The Haggadah is in fact a separate text.]
2. [A customary practice for Passover.]
3. [At the end of the fast of Yom Kippur, the Neïla is the closing prayer, when God grants forgiveness—or doesn't. The reference is used here to humorous effect.]
4. ["Blessed be the woman who birthed you": this informal expression is a common tribute to women in Spain.]
5. [Luke 23:34, New Testament, King James Bible. This is a crucial dialogue in the novel, addressing the reconciliation between the Jewish and the Christian religions.]

Mazaltob, Chapter 11

1. [This account is based on true events. See Introduction. Archives of the AIU, Maroc LXIV. E. 980. April 20, 1893.]
2. ["Boys" in Spanish.]
3. From Targum Hebrew: "May they be auspicious beginnings."

Mazaltob, Chapter 13

1. [The Algeciras Conference (January 16–April 7, 1906) was an international conference of European powers and the United States to discuss France's relationship to Morocco.]

Mazaltob, Chapter 15

1. [A reference to *The Sorrows of Young Werther* by Goethe.]
2. [The Viaticum is part of the Last Rites in the Catholic Church.]

Mazaltob and the Rise of the Modern Sephardi Novel

1. This essay examines the genre of the novel in the Maghreb. For a comparable study in the Mashreq, see the work of Lital Lévy on Esther Azharī Moyal and her activities as journalist, essayist, and literary translator: "Arab Jewish intellectuals and the case of Esther Azharī Moyal (1873–1948)" in *The Making of the Arab Intellectual: Empire, Public Sphere and The Colonial Coordinates of Selfhood,* ed. Dyala Hamzah (New York: Routledge, 2012).
2. Sadia Lévy et Robert Randau: *Rabbin*, G. Havard et fils, Paris 1896. Sadia Lévy co-wrote the novel *Rabbin* with Robert Randau, one of the founders of the Algerianist movement whose mission was to portray the local culture and landscapes of Algeria in order to promote a specifically French Algerian literature. Like *Mazaltob*, a section

of *Rabbin* is situated in Tetouan, a town from which hailed a large section of the Jews of Oran.

3. Edward W. Said, *Orientalism,* 25th anniversary edition, (New York: Vintage Books, 1994), 2–3.

4. "His chin was now decorated with a goatee beard, he wore a pince-nez and a long frock-coat and carried a glove like a roll of papyrus in his hand. The Romanians, the Egyptians, the Turks may hate the Jews. But in a French drawing room the differences between those peoples are not so apparent, and a Jew, making his entry as though he were emerging from the desert, his body crouching like a hyena's, his neck thrust forward, offering profound "salaams," completely satisfies a certain taste for the oriental." Marcel Proust, *Remembrance of Things Past,* Vol. III, trans. Scott Moncrief and Terence Kilmartin, revised by D.J. Enright (Modern Library, 1992), 253.

   The same trope of the Jew *qua* Oriental appears also in *Daniel Deronda* (1876) by George Eliot. The eponymous hero Daniel, who is Jewish, is associated throughout the novel with Prince Camaralzaman, a character from the *Arabian Nights*. (See for instance *Arabian Nights,* Chapter 16 [Penguin Classics, 1995], 184.)

5. The mellah is known as *Judería*—its Spanish name—in Northern Morocco.

6. Another archetypal example of whiteness as overdetermined in Orientalist art is Ingres's well-known *Odalisque with Slave* (c. 1842).

7. The phrase is from Susan Martin-Marquez, whose shrewd analysis I have followed here. Susan Martin-Marquez, *Disorientations, Spanish Colonialism in Africa and the Performance of Identity.* (New Haven: Yale University Press, 2008).

8. Ibid, 135.

9. See Eric Fournier, *La Belle Juive, d'Ivanhoé à la Shoah* (Champ Vallon, 2012).

10. Although Mary was Jewish, as the mother of Jesus, she is a key figure in Christianity.

11. I have closely adhered here to Nadia Malinovich's analysis in her informative article "Littérature populaire et romans juifs dans la France des années 1920," *Archives Juives* 1 no. 39 (2006): 46–62.

12. "Jewish soul", "Jewish race", "Jewish atavism."

13. Born in Narbonne, Benjamin Crémieux (1888–1944) was descended from an old Jewish family from the Midi. Arrested by the Gestapo in Marseilles, he was executed by the Nazis in Buchenwald in 1944.

14. Nordau, who was himself a doctor and a student of Lombroso, wrote a book titled *Degeneration* (1892) in which he recorded common traits he had observed among writers, thinkers, and artists—traits which were both a cause and a symptom of fin-de-siècle degeneration provoked by rapid urbanization and the industrial revolution. Nordau later became an ardent Zionist and a close friend of Theodor Herzl. He wrote another book titled *Musklejudentum* (1903) in which he advocated the regular practice of gymnastics for Jews in the future state he envisioned for them.

15. A modernizing movement, the Wissenchaft des Judentums grew out of the Haskalah, or Jewish Enlightenment, a late eighteenth-, nineteenth-century intellectual movement among the Jews of Central and Eastern Europe.

Notes

16. See Brenna Moore, "Philosemitism Under a Darkening Sky: Judaism in the French Catholic Revival (1900–1945)," *The Catholic Historical Review* 99, no. 2 (2013), 262–297.
17. Peguy's most important work, *Notre Jeunesse*, was published in 1910.
18. Raissa Maritain's husband Jacques Maritain (1882–1973) was a French Catholic philosopher who authored more than sixty books.
19. Mikhaïl Bakhtine, *The Dialogic Imagination: Four Essays*, trans. Caryl Emerson and Michael Holquist (University of Texas Press, 1981), 358.
20. Blanche Bendahan. *Poèmes en short*, préface de Paul Reboux, (Paris: éditions Renée Lacoste, 1948), 6.
21. Susan G. Miller was the first to point this out in her article "Gender and the Poetics of Emancipation: The Alliance Israélite Universelle in Northern Morocco, 1890–1912," in *Franco-Arab Encounters: Studies in Memory of David C. Gordon*, eds. Carl Brown and Matthew S. Gordon (Beirut, Lebanon: American University of Beirut, 1996).
22. Elisa Chimenti, *Le sortilège et autres contes séphardites*. (éditions marocaines et internationales, Tangier, 1964).
23. Alphonse de Lamartine, *Graziella* (Paris, 1852).

Further Reading

Alcalay, Ammiel. *After Jews and Arabs, Remaking Levantine Culture*. Minneapolis: University of Minnesota Press, 1993.

Blanche Bendahan. *Poèmes en short*, préface de Paul Reboux, (Paris: éditions Renée Lacoste, 1948), 6.

Benichou Gottreich, Emily and Schroeter, Daniel, ed. *Jewish Culture and Society in North Africa*. Bloomington: Indiana University Press, 2011.

Benkada, Saddek. "Blanche Bendahan (1893–1975), être écrivain, femme et juive à Oran dans l'entre-deux-guerres (1919–1939)," Société d'Histoire des Juifs de Tunisie, Colloque "Les Juifs du Maghreb de l'époque colonial à nos jours—histoire, mémoire et écritures du passé," Paris, Sorbonne du 3 au 6 novembre 2008.

Dugas, Guy. *La littérature judéo-maghrébine d'expression française*. Paris: éditions de l'Harmattan, 1991.

Even-Levy, Yaël. *The Poetics of Identity in Judeo-Maghrebi Poetry: The Poetry of Sadia Lévy, Ryvel, and Blanche Bendahan*. Ann Arbor: University of Michigan, 1998.

Garzón, Jacobo Israel. *Los judíos hispano-marroquíes (1492–1973)*. Madrid: Hebraica ediciones, 2008.

Katz, Ethan, Moses Leff, Lisa, and Mandel, Maud, ed. *Colonialism and the Jews*. Bloomington: Indiana University Press, 2017.

Leibovici, Sarah. *Chronique des juifs de Tétouan (1860–1896)*. Paris: Maisonneuve et Larose, 1984.

Levy, Lital. "Partitioned Pasts, Arab Jewish Intellectuals and the Case of Esther Azharī Moyal (1873–1948)." In *The Making of the Arab Intellectual (1880–1960): Empire, Public Sphere and the Colonial Coordinates of Selfhood*, edited by Dyala Hamzah. New York: Routledge, 2012.

Miller, Susan Gilson. "Gender and the Poetics of Emancipation: The Alliance Israélite Universelle in Northern Morocco (1890–1912)." In *Franco-Arab Encounters*, edited by L. Carl Brown and Matthew Gordon. Beirut: American University of Beirut Press, 1996.

Roumani, Judith. *Francophone Sephardic Fiction: Writing Migration, Diaspora, and Modernity*. Washington: Rowman and Littlefield, 2022.

Shreier, Joshua. *Arabs of the Jewish Faith: The Civilizing Mission in Colonial Algeria*. New Brunswick: Rutgers University Press, 2010.

Stein, Sarah Abrevaya. *Saharan Jews and the Fate of French Algeria*. Chicago: University of Chicago Press, 2014.

The Tauber Institute Series for the Study of European Jewry

JEHUDA REINHARZ, *General Editor*
CHAERAN Y. FREEZE, *Associate Editor*
SYLVIA FUKS FRIED, *Associate Editor*
EUGENE R. SHEPPARD, *Associate Editor*

The Tauber Institute Series is dedicated to publishing compelling and innovative approaches to the study of modern European Jewish history, thought, culture, and society. The series features scholarly works related to the Enlightenment, modern Judaism and the struggle for emancipation, the rise of nationalism and the spread of antisemitism, the Holocaust and its aftermath, as well as the contemporary Jewish experience. The series is published under the auspices of the Tauber Institute for the Study of European Jewry—established by a gift to Brandeis University from Dr. Laszlo N. Tauber—and is supported, in part, by the Tauber Foundation and the Valya and Robert Shapiro Endowment.

For the complete list of books that are available in this series,
please see https://brandeisuniversitypress.com/series/tauber

BLANCHE BENDAHAN
YAËLLE AZAGURY and FRANCES MALINO, editors
Mazaltob: A Novel

JEHUDA REINHARZ and MOTTI GOLANI
Chaim Weizmann: A Biography

*SCOTT URY and GUY MIRON, editors
Antisemitism and the Politics of History

JEREMY FOGEL
Jewish Universalisms: Mendelssohn, Cohen, and Humanity's Highest Good

STEFAN VOGT, DEREK PENSLAR, and ARIEH SAPOSNIK, editors
*Unacknowledged Kinships: Postcolonial Studies and
the Historiography of Zionism*

JOSEPH A. SKLOOT
First Impressions: Sefer Hasidim and Early Modern Hebrew Printing

*MARAT GRINBERG
The Soviet Jewish Bookshelf: Jewish Culture and Identity Between the Lines

*A Sarnat Library Book